MW01256807

That Which Was Lost

Amish Secret Widows' Society

Book 10

Samantha Price

Chapter 1

It is the glory of God to conceal a thing:
but the honour of kings is to search out a matter.
Proverbs 25:2

Ettie pottered about in the garden planting the seeds that her younger friends, Silvie and Maureen, had given her the night before. At just over eighty and no longer spritely, getting down on her knees was both time-consuming and painful, but the promise of new flowers in the summer powered her through. Besides, she always loved the smell of spring; it told a story of rebirth, which at her age was always reassuring.

Ettie often wondered if her life had grown too comfortable, raised as she was to believe boredom inspired sin in the young and led to the first rung on the journey to dementia in the old. But surrounded by her friends, young and old, Ettie enjoyed comfort. Having just conquered a bad case of pneumonia she was determined to enjoy whatever time God had blessed her with.

After putting her gardening tools away, Ettie prepared herself a cup of meadow tea. She settled down in her couch to enjoy a quiet moment before her sister, Elsa-May, came back from town. A loud knock on the door sounded, which made her jolt and spill a little tea into her saucer. "*Ach nee.*" She wasn't expecting any visitors or mail this late in the day. "Give an old girl a minute," she called out, pushing herself out of her comfortable spot.

When she opened the door and faced her caller, she was glad she'd set her cup on the table on her way to the door. "It's you. Is it really you?" Late afternoon sunlight shone through the woman's blonde hair, giving her a golden halo. "Myra."

"*Mamm*, you'll catch flies if you don't close your mouth." Myra's mouth formed a smile, but no hint of a smile touched her eyes. "Any chance I can come in or should I stand here in the garden?"

Ettie's heart pounded in her chest. "You wouldn't get away with being so cheeky if your *vadder* were still alive." She gulped on the lump forming in her throat. "Come in."

Myra passed her mother and entered the house, carrying a suitcase close to her side.

Ettie looked down at the suitcase. "How long's it been?" She stood back, palms on cheeks, still gaping.

"I know." Myra lowered her head before looking at her mother. "Too long. I'm sorry, *Mamm*. It never seemed the right time to contact you."

Once Myra set her suitcase on the floor, Ettie put both hands on her daughter's shoulders. "I think it was at your *vadder's* funeral, and I haven't seen you since."

"Oh, *Mamm,* it's so good to see you." Myra wrapped her arms around Ettie, and Ettie gave her daughter the first hug in decades.

Once the emotional reunion ended, Ettie stepped back, now practical and curious. She glanced again at Myra's suitcase. "You've come to stay?"

"For a while if that's okay."

Ettie bit her lip. She had only half the say in the household since she shared with her sister, Elsa-

May. "We've only two bedrooms in this small *haus*. You'll have to share with me."

Myra's hands shook, and her eyes were a swollen, ruddy mess, as though she'd been crying for some time.

"Sit down on the couch." Ettie waved her through into the living room. "Let me get you something to drink and eat. Did you drive far?"

"*Mamm,* don't fuss. You still have the compulsive need to feed people. I need to tell you something." When they sat, Myra said, "I need to talk to you before we do anything else. It's important, and I want to get it out of me and tell someone who won't patronize me."

Ettie could sense fear; Myra's presence had made the room sizzle with tension. "You're worrying me. How bad is it? Are you ill?"

"No, no. Well, recent events haven't helped my well being." Myra's eyes glazed over after giving a large sigh. "I don't know if I should have come, but I've nowhere else to turn."

They sat together in silence for a few more

moments before Ettie said, "Just tell me what happened and start at the beginning."

Myra remained silent.

The tense atmosphere weighed heavily on Ettie as the seconds passed like hours. "Whatever it is, I'm sure I can help you."

"Oh." Myra's tears fell down her cheeks. "I thought you could help, but now I'm not sure it was a good idea. I shouldn't show up like this and expect you to help me after I haven't spoken to you in years."

Ettie reached onto her coffee table and plucked out several tissues from a box. "Here." Ettie handed her the tissues. "Of course, you should. Now tell me, let me help you. Blow your nose, take a deep breath, and when you're ready, put this old woman out of her misery."

Myra cleaned herself up and inhaled deeply. "Peter, my husband of ten years, has vanished."

Ettie frowned; she hadn't known that her daughter had married. The rift between them had been great. The tragedy to bring her back must have been greater. "What do you mean by vanished?"

"He's gone; he's disappeared," Myra said.

Ettie saw her daughter's heart break before her eyes, and every instinct in her body hummed, like plucked strings on a guitar, urging her to do something, to fix things. All she could do was hold Myra's hand. "What did the police say?"

"They think I'm a sad, stupid middle aged woman. They think Peter's found a younger woman and run off with her."

Ettie wiped the tears from Myra's cheek. "Did they do anything useful? Like, check into his friends or extended family? His work colleagues?"

Myra rubbed her face. "Peter maintained that he was estranged from his family. He never asked me about my family and I never asked him about his." Myra dragged her fingers back through her hair.

Ettie nodded. "What have the police done?"

"Oh, I don't know, *Mamm*. And they washed their hands of the investigation, so I'm unlikely to find out."

"How could they? He's still missing."

"Oh, *Mamm*, it's so much worse than that."

"Worse, how?"

"They said his birth certificate, the one he used for our marriage, is fake." Myra stood and paced up and down, her tears relentless. "Who the hell did I marry?"

"People don't just up and vanish, Myra. He's out there somewhere." Ettie's mouth was suddenly dry. She thought of what Detective Crowley would do. "Did they track his cell phone, his credit cards, that sort of thing?"

"He didn't like to use credit cards. We had one that was in my name, and he used a pre-paid cell, which they couldn't track for some reasons. He committed no real crime according to them, so they said there are no more leads for them to follow. Without a real identity, they have nothing to go on."

Ettie didn't want to ask her next question, but had to broach the subject. "Do you think Peter had anything to do with his own disappearance?"

Myra snapped her head around. "No! I can't

believe anything bad about him, I won't."

Ettie stood, grabbing her daughter's hands to stop her from pacing, "I had to ask you."

Myra rested her head on Ettie's shoulder. "I want him back."

Ettie patted Myra's back while she thought things through.

Myra stepped away from Ettie and plucked more tissues from the box.

"Fake birth certificate, you say?" Ettie didn't like the sound of that. What kind of man uses a fake birth certificate to get married? A bigamist? A criminal on the run? "What about his passport or his driver's license? Surely one of those would turn up something."

"No, he had no passport, and his driver's license had been secured with his fake birth certificate." Myra shrugged. "There's no record of a Peter Davis. Well, there are loads of men named Peter Davis, it's a common name, but none is my Peter. My husband simply doesn't exist anymore." She frowned at her mother. "I've been married for ten years to someone who does not exist, and I don't know what to do about it. And worse, I don't know where he is or what's happened to him. Did I tell you most of his things are gone from the house?"

Ettie shook her head.

Chapter 2

*And without controversy great is the
mystery of godliness:
God was manifest in the flesh, justified in the Spirit,
seen of angels, preached unto the Gentiles,
believed on in the world, received up into glory.*
1 Timothy 3:16

Ettie sent Myra up for a bath and wondered how she would break the news of Myra's sudden visit to Elsa-May. While she prepared fried chicken and creamed potatoes, Ettie heard the taxi stop in front of the house. She took a deep breath and went to meet Elsa-May at the front door.

"Don't just stand there; help me with these bags," Elsa-May ordered as she walked up the front steps with hands full of grocery bags.

"*Jah*, I will, but just set them down before you go into the house; I need to tell you something."

Elsa-May promptly set her bags down and eyed Ettie carefully. "What's wrong?"

11

"Well, nothing really. It's just that Myra's come to stay for a bit."

Elsa-May's eyebrows rose so high that they nearly touched the front of her prayer *kapp*. "Myra, your Myra?"

Ettie nodded.

"What's that girl doing here after all this time?" Elsa-May asked.

"Hush, she's having a bath."

"That's not what I mean, Ettie. She and her *schweschder* haven't called or visited in years, so why now?" Elsa-May's lips formed a straight, disapproving line.

Ettie's eyes dropped from her sister's face onto the bags of food. "She's only here for a reason; she's in trouble. Come in, and I'll tell you all that she told me."

Both ladies carried the food into the house. While Ettie continued cooking dinner, Elsa-May put the food away.

"It's an intriguing story," Elsa-May said once Ettie had told her everything. They sat with hot tea at the kitchen table. Elsa-May leaned over the table and whispered, "She can't stay here. We've no room; the *haus* is barely big enough for the two of us. See if she can stay with Emma."

"*Nee*, I can't do that. She can sleep in my room with me."

Elsa-May's mouth turned down to form a scowl.

"What else can I do, Elsa-May? She's my *dochder,* and I haven't seen her for so long."

Rubbing her chin, Elsa-May asked, "Well, what do you think the bishop would have to say about her staying here?"

Ettie pressed her lips together. "The Yoders had Sam stay with them when he was on *rumspringa.* He stayed with them for two weeks. I'm putting my foot down, Elsa-May. This *haus* is half mine, and she's staying."

Elsa-May glared at Ettie for a moment before relenting with a nod.

"Let's try to figure things out before Myra comes down," Ettie said.

"Whichever way you look at it Peter is guilty of

something," Elsa-May said with a snarl. "If most of his clothes are missing it doesn't look like foul play."

"*Jah,* he must be a conman or a trickster, but what was his con? And why leave now after ten years with Myra? On the other hand, was Peter killed? Someone killed Peter for some reason and had to get rid of all trace of him. But murderers dispose of bodies, not identities. Who would bother, and why would they care about every tiny detail?"

"Stop, Ettie. You're going off on too many tangents, sounding like a mad woman. You need to keep a level head. Intelligent information is what we need."

The table was set and food ready to eat by the time Myra came downstairs wearing a blue robe and her hair in a towel turban. Her makeup gone, she was a gaunt shadow of the young, strong-willed daughter who ran away determined to make a life away from the Amish.

With a lump in her throat, Ettie remembered her little girl in plain dress, apron and prayer *kapp*.

"You're right on time, my girl, and you look so much better." Ettie dished out the food onto the center of the table.

"I don't feel better, but thanks." Myra pulled out a chair slowly as if the effort were too much. She sat down, then leaped out of her chair when she saw Elsa-May in the corner of the kitchen. "*Ant* Elsa." She hurried to her aunt and gave her a tight hug.

Elsa-May patted Myra on the shoulder. "I keep telling you it's Elsa-May. I don't call you Myr, do I?"

A girlish giggle sprang from Myra when she stepped back. "Still the same, I see."

Ettie coughed to hide her emotion at seeing her feisty child reduced to a vulnerable adult.

When they were all seated at the table, Myra said, "This all looks delicious, *Mamm,* although a sandwich would have done the job. You didn't need to go to so much trouble."

"No trouble, we have to eat too." They shared eye contact for a moment and a glimmer of a smile.

"I'll find some cider." Ettie stood and took a few steps toward the cold box before turning back. "Or would you prefer ginger beer?"

"Do you have wine? I think I've earned a glass," Myra said.

"We don't have any wine. Cider's the best we can offer," Elsa-May said.

After Ettie had poured the cider into the glasses, Ettie and Elsa-May closed their eyes in a silent prayer of thanks to God for the food.

When they opened their eyes, Elsa-May said, "Eat up, Myra, you'll need your strength for what's to come."

Myra looked at all the food. "Sorry, I'm so tired. I lost my appetite."

Ettie said, "You're no good to yourself or Peter if you starve to death. Besides, an empty stomach leads to an ..."

"An empty head. I remember." Myra sighed and ripped a chunk of fried chicken from the bone. "I never could get my food to taste as good as yours, *Mamm*."

After dinner, they took tea into the living room.

"What about his work?" Ettie asked, winding her fingers around the strings of her prayer *kapp*. It helped her to concentrate. "Surely there's paperwork there. They must know him; didn't they pay him, didn't he make friends? They might be able to help you find him."

"The place where he said he worked told the police that they have never had a Peter Davis working for them. Ten years he claimed he worked for that company, yet he never attended one Christmas party. He always said that he didn't like anyone there and preferred to spend time with me." Myra's eyes glazed over. "We were both loners; we only had each other. I suppose I should have thought it odd."

"Don't you feel this is your fault? Why would anyone suspect he lied about his job because he didn't like their parties?" Ettie said.

Myra nodded, sniffed back more tears, and blew her nose for the second time since dinner. "Thanks, *Mamm*. I knew you'd keep me rational, you always did." She grabbed her mother's hands in hers. "Please help me find him. The police wrote him off as a conman, a cheat because of his falsified birth certificate. They said he left me, and I should get on with my life. How do they expect me to do that?"

Elsa-May cleared her throat and asked, "Did he take any money?"

Myra shook her head. "No. He always had his money in my name; he said that it was better that way for tax. Even the house was in my name."

"His name was on nothing?" Elsa-May frowned.

"It's not so unusual, Aunt Elsa-May. Women are considered equals away from the Amish community."

"Women aren't less than men in the community, Myra." Elsa-May's voice rose.

Ettie put up her hand and glared at Elsa-May. "That's a subject for another time, not now." She looked back at her daughter. "So he has nothing in his name, and everything was in your name?"

Myra nodded.

The two elderly ladies stared at each other and exchanged knowing looks. They both knew that they needed the help of Detective Crowley.

A knock on the door made them all jump.

"Hello?" Maureen poked her head through the front doorway.

"Come in, Maureen," Ettie called out.

Maureen, their young friend who was also a widow, sat in the living room and was told of Myra's story.

"Does Crowley know?" Maureen asked.

The elderly ladies shook their heads.

Myra straightened her back. "Crowley? Ronald Crowley? Is he still in the area?"

"You know him?" Elsa-May asked.

"I knew him. It was a long time ago now. I didn't even think of contacting him," Myra said.

"Will you visit him tomorrow, Maureen, and have him call on us?" Elsa-May asked.

"*Mamm*, surely we can go see him," Myra said.

"*Nee*, he'll come and see us," Ettie insisted.

Maureen left without saying why she'd visited.

Elsa-May rose to her feet. "I'll be off to bed." She patted Myra on the arm. "We'll figure this out, my girl, but you must be strong."

Myra wiped her tears away. "Strong? I'll do my best, Aunt Elsa." Myra giggled at using half of Elsa-May's name once more.

Elsa-May shook her head at Myra's cheekiness. Ettie knew her daughter was trying to make herself feel better by having a light-hearted moment.

"We've only a small *haus*, Myra, I'm afraid you'll have to sleep in my room," Ettie said once her sister was out of the room.

"I can sleep on the couch if that's okay. I don't want to go home and be all alone."

"The couch won't be a *gut* place to sleep," Ettie said.

Myra bounced a little on the couch. "It feels soft and comfy. It'll be fine."

Ettie smiled, grateful that her nephew, Bailey, recently bought them the couch after she'd been sick. Before that, they only had hard wooden chairs. "Bailey bought this couch for me." Guests had always complained about the chairs, but Elsa-May and she were used to them.

"You say Bailey used to be in the FBI?" Myra asked.

Ettie nodded. "I know you're thinking he might be able to help, but we keep him out of things as much as we can. He's had too much trauma in his life already."

Myra looked down at her hands.

"We'll figure it out and find Peter. Don't you worry about a thing," Ettie said.

"I know, *Mamm*, that's why I'm here. I know you and Elsa-May are good at this kind of thing."

Chapter 3

Let us hear the conclusion of the whole matter:
Fear God, and keep his commandments:
for this is the whole duty of man.
Ecclesiastes 12:13

The earliest Crowley could make it was the following afternoon. He picked up Maureen on the way to Ettie's house and all the widows were waiting for them when they arrived. The widows including, Emma and Silvie were seated with cups of iced tea, a hot pot of coffee, and plenty of iced lemon cake placed before them.

He couldn't keep the smile off his face when he saw Myra. She was many years older than when he had last seen her. There were small wrinkles around her eyes and her skin wasn't as firm, but she was still a beautiful woman. Myra leaned into him and gave him a slight hug. Embarrassed at the widows watching them, he gave her a gentle pat on the back.

"Thanks for coming," Myra said to him.

"I know your mother and your aunt quite well." Crowley sat and saw all the food. He waved his hand to dismiss the feast. "Just water for me, please, Ettie. I'm off sugar at the moment."

"But it does get the energy up," Myra and Maureen said together. They sniggered at one another for quoting one of Ettie's many sayings.

Ettie smirked at the girls and frowned at Crowley. She handed around the plate of cake. "Eat, Crowley. There's work to do, and I want us all well fed."

Detective Crowley took a piece of cake, and after he had taken a mouthful, he placed it back down on the plate in front of him and took his pen and notepad from his inner coat pocket. Crowley wore a concentrated expression, along with his Columbo trench and well-worn shoes. He glanced up at the china clock, which sat on top of a bureau between two small embroidered Scriptures. "I have an appointment to keep after this."

"Right, best get on with it," Elsa-May said. "In

brief, Myra's husband disappeared as if he never existed and her local police aren't interested."

Crowley rolled his eyes and put his pen and pad back in his pocket. "Maybe he's gone off with another woman." He turned to Myra. "Sorry, but we see hundreds of these cases." He leaned toward Ettie. "We recently dealt with a very similar case and found the gentleman was with another lady. We wasted many hours of already over-stretched manpower, and spent good money out of a limited budget. I can understand why the police department washed their hands of the whole thing."

"No," Myra shouted. "He wouldn't have gone off with another woman." Myra nearly dropped her plate on the coffee table. "Mother, show him."

Crowley's eyes widened, and he attempted to apologize, but Ettie raised her hand. "Stop. You're theorizing without details. My fault; let me enlighten you of the facts. Thankfully, I noted them down, and I think you'll agree they're confounding." Ettie offered Crowley the list, which bullet-pointed the facts that Myra had given her. "You can read through it while you eat." Ettie pointed to his ignored slice of cake.

Crowley shook his head, took a large bite of cake and while reading, he both chewed and slurped on coffee. Once finished, he set the list on the table. Everyone in the room held their breath, hoping for some professional insight. "I maintain my original theory, I'm afraid. This man is a conman, pure and simple. If you research his finances, I bet you'll find debts built up under this fake name. Now he's off to do the whole thing again elsewhere, with a new name and a clean slate. Sorry, Myra, wish I could tell you something else, but that's my professional opinion. If he's got away for so long with a false identity, he won't think twice about creating another one." Crowley hated breaking bad news, but he always thought it best that it be said quickly as one would rip off a band-aid.

"I disagree." Ettie peered at her daughter, who appeared close to crumbling. "Why has no one in his office heard of him? Something's wrong, Detective, something else." She placed her palm over Myra's hand. "We'll get to the bottom of this on our own if we need to, but you could help us enormously in your line of work if you had a mind to, Detective."

"You're not alone," Maureen declared to Myra. "I'll help in whatever way I can."

"Me too," Emma said.

The widows shot a joint scowl at Crowley.

"You've always helped us before." Elsa-May narrowed her eyes at Crowley.

Detective Crowley took a deep breath. "Stop, please. I couldn't investigate this anyway; it's not my case. And we can't nose into people's finances, backgrounds, and any other details, without it being one of our cases. It can get in the way more often than not in my line of work, but it's the law."

Silvie sniped, "We aren't interested in the trials of being a detective. We invited you here as a friend who might want to help us in this matter."

"You have access to the records that we can't access. You don't have to 'officially' take the case." Ettie winked at the detective. "If you know what I mean."

The detective sat silently with his lips down-turned.

Elsa-May studied the detective before she stood up. "If you can't help us, we won't hold you up. Women have greater instincts than men, and it's no more evidenced than in this case."

With coffee in hand Crowley stood. "A bit sexist, don't you think?" Crowley walked to the door and left his cup on the walnut dresser in the hallway. "I'd help if I thought it would make a difference." Crowley bowed his head as he stepped outdoors. "If you turn up something a little more concrete, give me a call."

He headed to the car disappointed that they weren't listening to him. The man had to be some kind of criminal if he was using a fake birth certificate and pretending to be someone else. The widows were normally intelligent and caught onto things quickly. As he slid into the driver's seat, he realized that their personal association with Myra was clouding their judgment. He reminded himself not to end up guilty of the same thing. Crowley started the engine, turned his car around, and headed toward the main road knowing that the widows would end up roping him in – they always did.

* * *

Elsa-May closed the door on Crowley and sat down with Myra and the other widows.

"So he's not going to help?" Myra asked.

"*Jah*, he will eventually," Ettie said.

Myra frowned and stared at the widows in turn. "He refused us."

"He's like that most of the time, but he'll come 'round. Always does," Maureen said.

The widows sniggered and nodded in agreement.

"How are you getting home, Maureen? Didn't Ronald drive you?" Myra asked.

"I'm driving her home," Silvie said.

"My horse needs new shoes I'm afraid. I haven't had time to get it done," Maureen explained.

"I've forgotten all about driving by horse and buggy, it's not as easy as picking up the keys and getting in a car," Myra said, already missing basic modern conveniences.

"If I had a man, my life would be easier. He could look after the horse and buggy and all those outside things." Maureen laughed then stopped herself. "Oh, I'm sorry, Myra."

Myra shook her head. "Don't be; it's okay."

Maureen learned forward and looked into Myra's face. "Getting back to Crowley. We just need to have some piece of information that intrigues him. At the moment, he thinks that Peter has run away with another woman, but as soon as we prove that he hasn't, Crowley will want to know more. Don't worry, you'll see."

"Right." Ettie took one last slurp of her coffee and set the cup down on the coffee table. "The plan is Maureen will bug Crowley into doing all he can from his end. I know he said he couldn't, but he doesn't need to do anything that might lose him his pension—just a little nosing about. I'm sure he'll look into Peter's life, his employer's details, his cell phone, or something. All of which we're unable to do ourselves."

Silvie clasped her hands in her tiny lap. "Flirt a little, Maureen."

Maureen's mouth fell open. "Hush, Silvie. I'll do no such thing."

The widows and even Myra sniggered.

Ettie turned her attention to Myra. "You go back to your house and take Emma and Silvie with you. You must look for clues."

Myra frowned, "I looked for something, but there's nothing, that's the problem. Anyway, I can't go back there with him still missing. I can't." Myra sobbed into her hands.

The widows looked at Ettie, who said, "All right, give us the address and we'll go without you."

Ettie ignored Myra's comments about there being nothing there, deciding she would have been too emotional to see rationally. "And then, we can search in the place where Peter used to work."

"Search how?" Myra shook her head. "They

deny ever meeting Peter remember, let alone employing him."

"Interview his boss, a few of his colleagues. And if one of us could access the boss's computer and take a look at the human resources files, it could be very revealing."

Myra groaned, exasperated by her mother's ideas. "It's useless, none of this will work."

"It will. You asked for help so give us a chance," Ettie snapped. "We need your support, not this constant whining."

"*Mamm*?" Myra's eyes widened.

"Sorry, but honestly. You have no one else on your side remember? At least pretend to value our efforts." Ettie pressed her lips together.

Myra gaped and slumped back into the couch. "I do; it's all so frustrating."

Elsa-May sat next to Myra and grabbed a hand to hold in her lap before looking at Ettie. "What will you be doing, Ettie, and what about me?"

Ettie rubbed her nose. "We're the oldest, can't walk far, much less run around after people or flutter our eyelashes. We'll work through the clues and find any missing details from here as and when evidence comes in."

Myra peered around at everyone. "Thank you. I appreciate your support. *Mamm's* so lucky to have you as her friends."

A moment of emotion passed between them, somehow intensifying the smells of lemon cake, coffee, and the glorious fresh lilies Emma and Silvie had brought with them.

Maureen said, "We'll do our best to find him for you."

Emma smiled. "We'll get to the bottom of all this, Myra, you'll see."

Chapter 4

Abstain from all appearance of evil.
1 Thessalonians 5:22

Plans changed as Ettie decided to go to Myra's house the very next day as Maureen had been called in to work.

Elsa-May stayed with Myra while Silvie, Emma and Ettie drove in the taxi towards Myra's house, which was a twenty minute drive.

Silvie asked Ettie, "Do you think we'll find anything at the house? I understand she's upset and didn't want to come along, but how are we supposed to know what to look for?"

"Please, just trust. We've all done this kind of thing before. We want to find proof of who he is, or was." Ettie spoke quietly, so the taxi driver wouldn't hear what they were saying.

Silvie continued, "It just doesn't add up. Something is obviously wrong, but first we have to figure out who Peter really is. Perhaps that will lead us to find out where he disappeared to."

"That's right," Ettie said.

"So what do we want to find? Fingerprints?" Emma asked.

"Exactly," Ettie replied as the blur of trees zipping by the car's windows reminded her of her youth: just another thing that had gone by too fast. "We just need to find something of Peter's to have tested. Remember Crowley?"

"We need to find something that will make him want to help?" Emma asked.

"*Jah*. He's still a detective; he'll be as fascinated by this whole thing as we are."

"He didn't seem to be. He as good as said that Peter ran off with another woman," Silvie said. "I could ask Bailey if he'd help."

"We'll keep Bailey out of this. He's already gone out on a limb for us one too many times. Crowley will help." Ettie believed that it was much more than just a Missing Persons case, and so would Crowley once they found proof. It wasn't just that a man had run away with another woman. Nothing added up. "Why would he keep all his money, including the house, in Myra's name?"

"It's clear he wasn't using her for money," Silvie said. "Wasn't taking advantage of her financially."

"I wonder what the story is behind the fake birth certificate. Could he be an illegal immigrant? I know it's hard for people from other countries to become citizens here, so maybe that's it," Ettie said.

"Hopefully we'll get clues at the house." Silvie smiled as the taxi pulled into the driveway of Myra's home. "Let's get what we came here for."

As Ettie closed the car door, she looked around the front lawn. Nothing seemed out of place in the slightest. The grass was well kept, the hedges were trimmed, and the house looked immaculate. The four large windows that dotted the front of the house were all in pristine condition and locked. Silvie tried opening them unsuccessfully as Ettie fidgeted with the keys on Myra's heavy keychain. She finally found the one that her daughter had verbally labeled as the front door key. "Ah, here it is."

When they stepped through the door, Ettie handed disposable gloves to Silvie and Emma so they wouldn't upset any evidence they found.

As Silvie pulled the gloves on, she said, "Will anything we find be able to be used as evidence since we're not the police?"

Ettie's gaze wandered to the ceiling for a moment. "Let's not get beyond ourselves. There's no crime, we're looking to find some clue to help Myra find Peter."

Emma nodded. "Yes, of course."

As Ettie scoured the kitchen for clues, Silvie shouted from upstairs. "Ettie, it looks like no man has ever even lived here."

Ettie made her way upstairs into the master bedroom to see what the fuss was about. "Well, Myra did say that most of his things were gone, didn't she?"

"Yeah, but look," Silvie said, pointing to an open closet. As Ettie peered in, she noticed there were hardly any clothes in there.

"I know she's your *dochder,* but are you sure she was ever even married? Maybe she just made him up as an excuse to distant herself from you," Silvie said as she opened and looked in drawers.

Ettie looked at Silvie in disbelief. "*Nee,* it wasn't that. We stopped talking long before her husband was ever in the picture. She left the community as a teenager, most likely before you were even born."

"I know, but something just doesn't add up. Either she made up his entire existence, or he did." The sound of truth in Silvie's assessment made Ettie's stomach turn. Why on earth would anyone falsify an identity for over ten years? The women continued looking through most of the house and had found nothing when Ettie was struck with the idea to look in the garage. Ettie instructed Emma to continue her search inside the house while she rummaged through the garage with Silvie.

"We need something with Peter's fingerprints. If he left something behind, it would probably be in here," Ettie said as she pulled up the sliding metal door of the two-car garage. The sound of metal scraping tore at the old woman's hearing. "I'm getting too old for this."

Silvie giggled at Ettie's words, but Ettie had been serious.

Once the door was completely up, they strolled into the garage. As Silvie looked around, Ettie searched through a stack of old, rusted car parts slumped against a corner of the room. It looked like a car had exploded, cooled off, and then all of its pieces landed in one area.

"Nothing here is useful, unfortunately." Just as those words left Ettie's lips, her eyes fell on the shining steel shaft of a golf club. A single club sat isolated in its golf bag, waiting to be collected and tested for fingerprints. "At last; I think this might work," Ettie said, holding up her newly discovered treasure in her gloved hand.

"Great. I'll have the taxi drop you back at your place, and then I'll take this down to the station and show Detective Crowley," Silvie said sweetly.

Ettie nodded in agreement, and after they had

collected Emma, the three women headed to the waiting taxi.

* * *

The next day, Ettie woke to the sound of someone banging on the front door. She jumped out of bed, hoping that Myra wouldn't wake. Walking past Myra asleep on the couch, she was glad to see she was fast asleep. She opened the door to see Crowley.

"Ettie, we just ran the prints through AFIS and got a match. They came back as belonging to a man named Preston Judge. Is he someone your daughter might know?"

"I'm not sure, Detective." Ettie rubbed her face; she was still half asleep. "Myra's asleep on the couch. Can I come and see you later today after we try to figure out who this man is?"

"Of course."

"Thank you. We all appreciate your help," Ettie said, satisfied that Crowley had been of some help.

Crowley peered over Ettie's head. "Could you tell Myra I said hello?"

"Of course, Detective."

Ettie closing the door startled Myra. "*Mamm*, was that Crowley?" Ettie saw the concern in her daughter's eyes as she walked toward her. "Did he get a match?" Myra asked.

"Yes, but the prints weren't Peter's. The fingerprints belonged to a person named Preston Judge."

"Preston? I've never heard that name before in my life." Her brow furrowed. "We just had the entire house repainted, so maybe one of the painters touched things in the garage. You did say the prints were found on a golf club in the garage?"

Ettie nodded. "That's right."

"The painters stored their things in the garage. One of them could easily have left the prints behind."

Ettie let out a disheartened sigh. "Well if that's the case, I suppose I should call Silvie. We have to find something else to test."

"*Mamm*, what about his toothbrush?" Myra said.

"You have his toothbrush?" Ettie frowned. That information might have been useful yesterday.

"It's at the house, on the bathroom sink. I remember seeing it after I realized most of his belongings were gone. I thought it odd he'd leave only that behind, but I didn't even consider it being of importance until just now."

Ettie wondered why they hadn't thought to look in the bathroom. "A toothbrush should work for DNA testing. Silvie said she'd stop by today and when she does, we'll go back to your house."

* * *

Two days later, Crowley knocked on Elsa-May and Ettie's door. Ettie ushered him into the living room where he sat in front of Myra, Elsa-May and Ettie.

"The DNA on the toothbrush was also a match to Preston Judge." He looked at Myra. "Peter Davis and Preston Judge have to be one and the same

43

person."

The three women looked at each other in silence.

Crowley continued, "After I received the hit from CODIS, I did some digging and found the last known residence of Mr. Judge. It's located about fifty miles southwest of here. I'm heading out there in the morning."

Ettie said, "Do you have any other information about him?"

"It seems he was in the military service years ago and that's how his fingerprints wound up in the system," Crowley said.

Myra scratched her head. "Peter never mentioned anything of the kind."

"Thank you so much, Detective," Elsa-May said.

"Anything I can do to help," he replied with sincerity in his voice. The detective left just as suddenly as he had arrived.

Myra was quiet and Ettie daren't say anything to her through fear it would end in tears.

Eventually, Myra took a deep breath. "It's like a nightmare, a bad dream. My whole life has been a lie." She looked across at her mother. "The last ten years of my life have all been for nothing. I don't even know the man I was married to."

Chapter 5

Wherefore receive ye one another,
as Christ also received us to the glory of God.
Romans 15:7

Crowley drove out to see what he'd find at the home of Preston Judge, Crowley knew by now it wasn't a simple instance of a missing person.

The beautiful homes and rural scenery filled him with a dread that he couldn't understand. "Where on earth is King Road?" Flipping through the maps and books that lined the passenger seat while he drove, Crowley grew frustrated.

"Take your next right. Turn now," his GPS shrieked. Swerving to make the turn, his car veered up a dirt road that led to his destination. A large, Victorian style home, which, according to Google maps, sat nestled in one corner of at least fifteen acres of land, came into view. He parked close to the front door and stepped out onto the property.

Approaching the front door, Crowley swept his gaze across the property. He rang the doorbell of the beautiful home, noting that homes like that came with a hefty price tag.

After less than a minute, the door swung open and a well-groomed woman said, "May I help you?"

The woman was of slight build with hair too dark for her face. Even Crowley could tell that the woman dyed her hair a shade too dark for her sallow complexion. Permanent worry lines etched into her forehead and in between her brows.

"Yes, Ma'am. I'm Detective Crowley." He showed his ID. "I wonder if I might talk to Preston Judge?"

"Is something wrong?" Panic swept across the woman's face.

"No, Ma'am. I was just hoping I could speak with him, if he's in."

"He's at work; he'll be home tonight."

Knowing she was too expensively dressed to be the help, Crowley asked, "Can I ask what relationship you have to Preston?"

"I'm his wife."

The puzzle assembled, piece by piece. The man had to be a bigamist. Crowley knew that he had to get inside and hopefully there would be some framed photos. He also knew that rich people often commissioned portraits, which they displayed in their homes. In his mind he held a picture of Peter Davis from the photo Myra had shown him days before. "Do you think we could speak inside?"

"Is that completely necessary? I assure you he's not here right now."

Mrs. Judge seemed nervous, but instincts told Crowley that he needed to get inside.

"I completely believe you, Mrs. Judge. I'd just like to see how beautiful this house is on the inside." Crowley did his best attempt at a friendly chuckle. "I've been admiring your house since I pulled off the main road." His eyes grew larger as he glanced through the open door. "It's truly marvellous. My wife would love a beautiful home like this." Crowley knew women were always more at ease with him when he pretended he had a wife.

"Well, I suppose it wouldn't hurt," she said with a smile. She led him through the living area and showed him a few of the rooms. "My husband and I fell in love with the house as soon as we saw it."

In the office, Crowley noticed a picture of a middle-aged man and Mrs. Judge. "What a lovely picture. Is that you and Preston?" he inquired.

"Yes, it was taken years ago." Mrs. Judge walked up to the picture. "It was on one of our trips to the Bahamas." After showing him two more rooms, Mrs. Judge said, "Anything else, Detective?"

He knew the truth. Preston Judge and Peter Davis were the same person. Myra's husband had been living a double life. Shaking off the disbelief and dread of telling Myra, he turned to the woman and said, "Thank you. I appreciate you letting me look around such a nice home."

"If it's urgent you could catch him at work."

Just as Crowley opened his mouth to speak, loud banging on the door echoed through the house.

"Excuse me a moment, Detective," Mrs Judge

said before she opened the door.

Two uniformed police officers, one male and one female, stood behind a man who was clearly a plainclothes detective. "Hello. Are you the wife of Preston Judge?"

"Yes. I'm Priscilla Judge." Her hand flew to her mouth. "Did something happen?" Fear vibrated through her words.

"May we come in?" the detective asked.

She opened her mouth, glanced back at Crowley and stepped aside to let them in.

Once they were inside the house, the detective introduced himself and showed his badge. "I'm afraid we've got some bad news. We're sorry to inform you this way, but your husband was found dead early this morning."

A chilling scream shot out of her mouth and she fell to her knees. Crowley reacted quickly, slowing her fall. Attempting to console the shattered woman, he held her in his arms and spoke calming words. "We'll find out what happened, I promise you."

"Are you a friend?" the other detective asked.

"Maybe we should talk outside," Crowley suggested as the female officer stepped in to take his place.

Priscilla Judge was left in the house comforted by the female police officer while Crowley walked outside to speak to the detective and the male officer. "I'm Detective Crowley. I know this isn't my jurisdiction, but I'm here following up on a Missing Persons case. A woman by the name of Myra Davis reported her husband missing recently. She claims that he vanished, taking most of his belongings with him. We DNA matched him to Preston Judge and the photo I've got of Peter Davis matches a photo of Mr. Judge that I found in the house here."

Detective Jenkins said, "Your missing person is this woman's husband? So he's a bigamist?"

"Yes. May I ask the cause of death?"

The other officer continued scribbling notes on a small pad. "Stabbed in the back; no sign of a struggle, which tells me he might have known the perpetrator."

Crowley raised his eyebrows. "Stabbed? Where was he found?"

"Not far from his office in an alley. As yet we haven't been able to locate any CCTV cameras in the area."

The younger officer continued, "According to his work colleagues he often used to go to the gym before work and this morning he never made it into work. We have the time of death at around eight this morning. His body was found in an alley near the gym. He must have been heading to his car. His wallet wasn't taken so we can rule out robbery as a motive."

"Hmm." Detective Crowley considered the possibilities. "I'm guessing there was no sign of a weapon?"

"We've got officers combing the area now." Detective Jenkins scratched his head and glanced back at the house before he said, "We haven't told Mrs. Judge yet, but the victim's face was pretty badly smashed in."

Crowley took a deep breath. "I think this case will just continue getting stranger. Preston was married to Myra Davis posing as her husband, Peter Davis; Peter Davis was using a fake birth certificate." Crowley felt sweat beading on his forehead thinking how he would break the news to Myra that not only was Peter a bigamist, now he was dead. He also had to wonder whether someone was trying to hide Peter's bigamy by destroying his face.

The two men walked away from Crowley. Crowley knew they didn't want to share the case with him. He watched and listened to them from a distance and could only make out a few muffled words.

Crowley listened for a few more minutes before he noticed Detective Jenkins approaching him.

"Hey, Crowley!" Crowley stood still and hoped that they weren't going to make investigations difficult for him. "We want to have a talk with Mrs. Davis if you could arrange that for us."

"Excuse me, Detective Jenkins, but with all due

respect, I think I should speak to her in my office so I've got a recorded interview. Her case falls under my jurisdiction." Crowley wasn't telling the full facts, but first thing when he got back to the office, he would take over the missing persons case officially. He didn't mean to be rude, but his many years on the force had solidified his iron disposition. He learned the hard way that nice guys finish last in his line of work.

"Yes, you're right. We didn't mean to step on your toes, Crowley. We would love to conduct this as a joint interview if that would satisfy your concerns."

Crowley thought through the matter carefully; a joint interview might be an advantage. "I'll speak with Mrs. Davis and bring her in tomorrow. I'll phone you in the morning and make a definite time. And, of course, you'll make the interview tapes available to me; and the tapes of the interview with Mrs. Judge and anyone else who might be pertinent?" Crowley knew he had to get as much information as possible so he could make sense of the whole thing.

After Jenkins agreed, Crowley asked all the questions about the Judge family that he could think of before leaving to tell Myra the terrible news. It was obvious that Preston Judge was leading a double life and that he had at least two wives; the question was: 'Did one of the wives kill him or have him killed?'

Crowley knew that he had to go back to Myra and break the news about her husband. Even though she hadn't identified the body as her husband, the DNA was a match. Without fingerprints and without visual identification they had to trust the DNA results that Preston and Peter were one and the same. He hated breaking news of death, especially when he knew the people involved.

An hour later, he knocked on Ettie's door and Myra opened it.

"Myra, I'm afraid it's bad news."

Myra crumpled onto the floor.

Ettie ran up behind Myra and looked up into Crowley's face. "Is he…?"

Crowley nodded. "I'm afraid so."

Myra looked up from the floor. "How?"

"Let's talk inside," Ettie said.

Both Crowley and Ettie helped Myra to the couch.

"How did he die?" Myra asked.

"I'm afraid that he was stabbed as he was leaving the gym."

"No, Detective, you've got the wrong man. Peter hated exercise. I could barely get him to go on a walk with me. Myra put her hands over her face and cried. After a while she wiped her eyes on tissues that Ettie had handed her and she said, "Ronald, there's something else, isn't there?"

"I'm afraid so. I've got more distressing news for you," Crowley said.

"Tell me." Myra's eyes fastened on to him.

"Preston Judge, which was your husband's real name, was living, well, married to another woman."

Myra looked at her mother. "No, it can't be possible; we were married for ten years. I'd know if there had been someone else."

"From what I know about the other wife, he was married to her for close to fifteen years. They live about an hour and a half drive from here."

"Did they have any children, Detective?" Ettie asked.

"From what the police told me, the woman has a son from a previous marriage. He's a grown man now, and he moved out on his own a couple of years ago." He looked at Myra. "I'm sorry to have to tell you all this bad news. The police from Radallston want to speak to you tomorrow."

"Did he suffer?" Myra asked through tears.

"I think it was fast," Detective Crowley said.

Elsa-May came into the room and sat with them. "I heard everything. Do they think Myra's a suspect, Detective?"

"In any case like this, we always look into the spouse first." Crowley cleared his throat. "In this case there are two of them."

"I understand. Where's Peter, can I see him?" Myra asked.

Crowley shook his head. "He's still having tests

run on him for evidence."

"When can I see him? I won't believe it until I see his body. What if it's not him and he's still out there?"

"Myra, I saw a clear photo of him at the house and I can tell you, he and Preston Judge are one and the same man." Crowley cleared his throat. "I'm afraid his face was damaged and he's no longer recognizable."

After Myra sobbed for a few more moments she asked. "Does his other wife know about me?"

"I'd say she does by now. I was talking to her when the police arrived to break the news of his death. I left when she was still with the police."

"So she must be his real wife, since he married me under a false name with fake papers." Tears flowed down Myra's cheeks.

"It would seem so. Would you be up to talking to them tomorrow? They've asked if I can bring you in for questioning."

"Give her a few days," Ettie said. "She's too distressed."

"No, I need to do this," Myra said. "Yes, I can go with you tomorrow. I'm just glad you'll be going with me."

"Will you be with her during questioning?" Elsa-May asked.

Crowley nodded.

Elsa-May folded her arms across her chest. "Will she need a lawyer?"

Crowley glanced at Myra before looking at Elsa-May. "I don't think so. It's just routine questions at this stage."

Chapter 6

All that the Father giveth me shall come to me;
and him that cometh to me I will in no wise cast out.
John 6:37

As light crept through his squinted eyes, Crowley tossed and turned in the morning sun. Shielding his eyes with a pillow, he looked over at the alarm clock by his bed. A slight frown broke across his stern face as he thought about what the day might bring. It had already been a strange start to his week. Would Myra have been capable of killing her husband? Could she have found out that he was a bigamist and done away with him? An image of Mrs. Judge loomed in his mind's eye; would she be capable of cold-blooded murder, or of hiring someone to kill her husband?

No, he decided, Myra would not be capable of such a thing. People never change that much. It had been almost an entire lifetime ago when he was close to Myra after she had left the Amish community. She was much younger than he, and she was always outgoing, fun, and absolutely beautiful. At times he wasn't able to believe that she might have had feelings for him, but his confidence was severely lacking. He wished it would have been different, but he always knew he never had a chance with her. Now, he had to face a harsh reality that Myra might be responsible—at least accused of—a homicide.

He struggled out of bed into the kitchen and flipped the switch on the coffee maker before he jumped in the shower. After his shower, with just a towel around his waist, he poured out a bowl of Froot Loops. He sat with a large mug of black coffee and spooned the colored cereal into his mouth, all the while knowing he should be eating something more substantial. Maybe he and Myra could stop to eat on the way, before heading to Randallston.

As he pulled up to Ettie's house, he noticed Myra was sitting on the steps, waiting for his arrival. She stood to her feet as he pulled into the driveway.

Opening the door, she smiled sweetly and

greeted him with a, "Good morning, Detective."

He tipped his hat and smiled. "How are you today, Ma'am?"

"So formal. You do remember we used to be friends, Ronald?"

The words felt like a fire, warming his cheeks to a rosy, red color. "Please, Myra. Don't call me that. Crowley, or Detective works fine."

Once she buckled her seat belt, Crowley's car moved away from the house.

Myra looked out her window, and said, "I should be dying inside, but I'm not."

The revelation punched the detective in his stomach. "Why, Myra? Was he a violent man?" *Did he do something to you, Myra? Did you punish him for it?*

"No, he was never violent."

"I was just curious to know if he has done anything to put you in a situation where you had to defend yourself."

"I would never harm my husband or anyone. Peter was unpredictable. Mostly we got along like a dream, but then he'd snap and become nasty for no reason at all. I was sure that he picked fights deliberately and it was after those times that he'd disappear for days, sometimes three or four. It all makes sense now."

"He'd pick a fight then disappear because it suited him to be elsewhere for a few days? You'd blame yourself for arguing with him, thinking the argument had sent him away to cool down?"

"That's right, that's how it was. But, I loved him. We didn't have many arguments except for those ones. I didn't sleep last night, I was piecing together all the little things."

Crowley glanced over at her. "I've never been married, but I've seen my share of marital problems when it escalates to domestic abuse."

Myra nodded and looked down.

"Myra, you and I were close once. I want to find out what's going on. I'm doing this for you, not because I'm a detective."

"Thank you." Her voice was weak, almost child-like.

Silence filled the car as they continued their journey. Crowley glanced at his watch and noticed they were ahead of schedule. "You hungry? I was in a hurry, so I never grabbed my morning coffee." He lied, he couldn't tell her he ate a bowl of froot loops and downed it with a mug of black coffee. "I'll treat you to some breakfast, if you'd like?"

Myra's eyes sparkled as the morning sun shone through the car window. "I'd like that."

* * *

"Would you like sugar or cream with your coffee, sir?"

"Both please," Crowley said to the waitress.

As the waitress handed him some creamers and packets of sugar, she turned to Myra and asked if she were ready to order.

"Yes, I'm ready," she said, looking up at the waitress. "I'll just have a lumberjack breakfast. Scrambled, bacon, and white toast, please."

Crowley browsed the daily newspaper as they

waited for their meals. "Well, it hasn't made the papers yet, but once their murder victim is linked to Peter, it's sure to be a big news story. Preston Judge was quite a wealthy man." He put the paper down and sipped at his coffee as he peered out through the windows. "Sure hope today continues to be a nice one."

"Peter wasn't a bad man, but I feel as though I don't know the person I was married to. We kept to ourselves and I don't really have anyone I could call a close friend. Peter didn't like to socialize and he didn't want me doing anything. I stayed home and sculpted, and the only time I went out was to go to art exhibitions or to buy things related to sculpting, such as tools."

Peter was stabbed and Myra has sculpting tools. Crowley didn't like thinking that way, but years of being a detective had made suspicion a habit. He had to ask Detective Jenkins what type of implement was used in the stabbing. "He kept you isolated?"

"I guess you could say that. Looking back, I

guess that was his plan. If we weren't out in public then no one from his other life would spot us."

The waitress interrupted and placed their meals before them.

Sympathy overwhelmed Crowley as he thought about what he'd just heard. A woman he wanted nothing more than to protect, was confessing to him that her murdered husband was controlling, on top of the fact that he was living a double life. Crowley wondered if Peter were also physically abusive. He knew women were often ashamed of being abused, and rarely admitted to being victims.

"Can you promise me that you don't know what happened to your husband whatever his actual name is? I do believe you, but I just need to look into your eyes when you tell me yourself." He smiled hoping his words would not offend her.

"The thing is, are you sure that the man found dead is really Peter?"

"I think we can safely say that he was Peter."

"I promise you I don't know anything about anything except that Peter disappeared and I had no idea about his other life. I don't know where he would've found the time, since he was mostly with me."

"He worked far away from home, didn't he?"

"He worked at Randallston and left early and came home late."

The detective nodded, case closed as far as he was concerned, especially with the missing days and finding out from the other detective that Mrs. Judge said that her husband worked away an awful lot. "There is one personal thing I'd like to ask you, if I may, Myra."

"Sure, what is it?"

"Why did you contact your mother to help you with this case?"

"Case?"

He shook his head and looked down. "I'm sorry; I'll rephrase that. Why did you turn to your mother when Peter went missing? You haven't been near the community in years. I've had contact with Ettie quite a bit over the years and I know you haven't seen her in ages."

"Excuse me?" Myra's eyes turned steely.

"I know that you two have been estranged for a long time. Why would she be the first person you contact after your husband goes missing?"

"My mother and I were close once, but she wouldn't go against my father or the community. There's no room for individuality in the community and if you don't fit in there's only one thing for it, you have to leave. The Amish say they have no pride, but they pride themselves in losing themselves and being a group." Myra waved her hand in the air. "People can't rid themselves of pride. They are proud of having no pride." Myra gave a small chuckle as she stared into her coffee. "My father was the worst, but it led to my mom and me no longer talking as well."

"I'm sorry to hear that. I hope I didn't open up any old scars. But still, why turn to her when this happened?"

"It's been so long since I needed anyone, and when I was young she was always that one person who would be there. I guess it's hard to trust someone new when you have that person, that rock, who will never turn you away."

"You can always find a second rock, though."

A faint blush highlighted Myra's cheeks as Crowley spoke.

As soon as they finished their breakfast, Crowley said, "Well, I guess we should get back on the road."

Once they were in the car, Crowley knew he had to prepare Myra for what was to come. "The detectives and officers working the Preston Judge case are going to look at you as a possible suspect. Don't tell them I mentioned that, and don't act like you think it. Just be yourself and be honest. They need to eliminate you as a suspect before they move on."

"Okay, I understand."

"Just make sure you're adamant that you have never heard of Preston Judge or his wife before because that's the truth. It's important that you don't lie though. I'm trusting you, so please, don't make me regret it."

Myra took a deep breath. "Ronald, I'm the victim here. I haven't done anything wrong; this has all happened to me."

"I'm sorry, Myra. I shouldn't have put pressure on you."

"I know it's your job, but I haven't done anything wrong."

Crowley nodded and knew that Myra was holding back tears. He was angry with himself for questioning her like he had. The car pulled into the Randallston station at noon. "Like I said, I'll be there next to you, just tell them what you know. I'll do what I can to help you through this."

Myra reached her right arm over and gave him a soft hug. "Thank you for being here for me."

The embrace left a warm sensation bubbling in Crowley's stomach. Despite the case, and the uncertainty that even he held onto, he couldn't explain the way he felt about Myra. He felt a loyalty to her that he didn't understand.

* * *

"I suspect Detective Crowley has filled you in on recent events?" Detective Jenkins said to Myra once they were in the interview room.

Myra nodded. "Of course."

Detective Jenkins read his notes then looked up at Myra. "I understand that you were married to one Preston Judge?"

Myra glanced over at Crowley who was sitting to her right. "I was married to Peter Davis; that's who I knew him as. I just found out that he was a bigamist, and I never suspected a thing. Although I'm not entirely convinced that this Preston fellow was my husband." Myra gave them all the information she could on Peter, where he told her that he worked and what he had told her of his past. She had also brought with her a handful of Peter's paperwork.

The officer in charge held up the paperwork including Peter's fake birth certificate. "Okay if we take copies of these?"

"Please do," Myra said.

The officer passed the paperwork to a young

policeman who had been standing at the back of the room. "Get two copies of each."

"Right away, sir," the young officer replied before he left the room.

Detective Jenkins turned his attention to Crowley. "There's been a development. We've found an abandoned car that was registered in Preston's name. Mrs. Judge swears she's never seen the car. It's a red SL500 2003 Mercedes-Benz."

Myra gasped. "That's Peter's car."

"We're going over it now for evidence." He looked down at his papers then up at Myra. "When was the last time you saw Preston?"

Myra took a deep breath. "Peter," she said with a mildly defiant look, "left for work one morning, and at about ten o'clock and I went to the mall. When I came back a couple of hours later, I noticed that his things had gone missing."

"What things?" Detective Jenkins made notes.

"Most of his clothes and everything. I'd bought a pair of shoes and when I went to put them in our closet, I noticed that most of his clothes were gone.

I couldn't work it out. We hadn't had an argument in a while, and there was no reason for him to leave me. I searched for a note, but didn't find one." Myra put her fingertips in her mouth.

Jenkins set his pen down. "You had regular arguments?"

Myra shrugged. "We had some misunderstandings as most couples do."

Jenkins tilted his head to the side. "How many would you say is 'regular'?"

"I don't know, about one a week, or a fortnight."

"And what would these arguments be about?" Jenkins asked.

"Peter would pick silly fights with me and then disappear for two days. That's why I couldn't work out why he'd disappeared this time when we'd had no fight."

Jenkins pushed himself back into his chair. "Fight? Would you say you had fights or arguments?"

"Well, I'd say arguments," Myra said.

"But you just said fight…"

"Stop this." Crowley leaned forward. "Myra is here to offer information to help this case. If she's not being arrested for anything I'll have to ask you to stop your harassment." Crowley glared at the officer who was acting like a cross-examining barrister rather than trying to gather pertinent information.

Jenkins picked up his pen and tapped it on the table. "I'm sorry, Myra. I found it odd that you used the word 'fight' and 'argument' as if they were the same thing."

Myra shrugged. "Peter never got physical if that's what you mean. He'd get angry but never got violent. And he'd only get angry right before he'd disappear. I suppose he was going back to his other wife."

"Were you ever suspicious that Peter might be having an affair or might have another family somewhere?"

"No, that would be the last thing I would ever have thought of. I trusted him completely. He was all I had, and I thought it was the same for him."

"What about his family? Did you have his family at your wedding?"

"We had a quiet ceremony; it was just a civil service. We were both estranged from our families. Well, I was from mine; he said that he never got along with his family and I believed him."

"Convenient," the detective said as he shuffled through his notes. "Where did you think he went when he was gone for days?"

"I don't know. I never asked him; I suppose that I didn't want to start another argument, I just wanted to move on."

Detective Jenkins looked up from his notes. "Did he ever have strange calls coming to the house?"

Myra screwed up her nose. "Never."

"Did you ever see anything strange on his cell phone or his email?"

Myra shook her head. "I never looked at either."

"Was there ever anything strange on the credit card bills; anything unaccounted for?"

"No, nothing like that. I told you, everything appeared normal to me. This was the last thing I ever expected," Myra asked.

"So, you never followed him?" Detective Jenkins tapped his pen on the table.

Myra frowned. "Never."

"You never knew or met anyone from his work?"

Myra shook her head.

"How did you know where he worked?"

"He told me where he worked. His pay was put into my bank account at the end of every month. I handled the money, paid the bills, that kind of thing."

"You don't work?"

"Peter didn't want me to work. I met him at an art gallery where I worked and once we got married, he insisted I stay home and concentrate on my sculpture. He convinced me I had talent." Myra looked at her hands in her lap. "I don't even know if that's true now."

After three hours of questioning, the interview was over. Crowley left Myra in the waiting room while he went back to find out about the murder weapon. Jenkins informed him that the victim was killed with a large knife, resembling a butcher's knife, and it had been wiped clean of prints. Crowley collected Myra and drove her back to Ettie's house.

Chapter 7

But now I have written unto you not to keep company,
if any man that is called a brother be a fornicator,
or covetous, or an idolater, or a railer, or a drunkard,
or an extortioner; with such an one no not to eat.
1 Corinthians 5:11

Myra found the front door to her mother's home was unlocked, which she was grateful for. She had staggered out of the detective's car and made it up the front steps to the house without falling over. Her knees were like jelly and getting a full breath of air was difficult between sobs.

Stumbling into the house, she headed for the kitchen hoping for a hot cup of tea and a chair to fall into, something to give her solace and support.

Ettie was sitting in her usual spot at the kitchen table and looked up from the newspaper when Myra entered. Elsa-May was drinking tea on the opposite side.

"What happened?" Ettie rushed to Myra's side

and began dabbing at the tears on Myra's face with a handkerchief.

"It was horrible, *Mamm*," Myra said, taking a seat at the kitchen table. Aunt Elsa-May reached out a hand and patted Myra's arm.

"How was the meeting with the police?" Elsa-May asked.

"You mean, how was the interrogation? There's nothing like being made to feel like 'the other woman' and a suspect at the same time."

"What do you mean, 'the other woman'?" Ettie asked.

"Well, I was the other woman because everyone acts as if I'm someone he was inappropriate with, and Peter's other wife was the 'real' one."

"The worst part was they had questions for me about his death. As if I'd know anything. I don't think I know anything about the man who was my husband, not even that he had another family!" Myra stared at Elsa-May's teacup.

"I'll make you a cup," Elsa-May said.

"It was awful," Myra continued. "They made

me feel so stupid as if I should have known my husband was cheating on me. I was too blinded by love to see the truth. And the worst part was that I was afraid to tell them how horrid he was at times because then they might've thought I had something to do with his death!"

"No way around that one, you're right," Ettie commiserated. "But why did they want to talk to you at all? Do they think you're a suspect?"

"Ettie, you heard Crowley say they have to eliminate the spouses as suspects before they move on," Elsa-May said firmly.

"I suppose so. He did say it was routine," Ettie said.

"I don't know, really. It was pretty routine stuff. Where was I during the time when he died, how often was he there, did he act unusually at all - that kind of thing."

Elsa-May set a steaming mug of tea in front of Myra and patted her shoulder. "So what did you say?"

"I just told them the truth of what had happened.

And no, of course, I didn't know he had another family! If I had, I would have kicked him out and let the other family have him! The worst part was that the detective kept tapping his pencil on the desk; tap, tap, tap. tap." Myra's finger tapped on the kitchen table illustrating the rhythm. "I could barely think straight with all that racket! It was like Chinese water torture! I swear if Detective Crowley hadn't been there with me I would've jumped out of my chair and admitted to anything just to get him to stop!"

"There, there, take a deep breath. You're getting all worked up again," Ettie whispered.

"And the way they kept asking me the same questions, over and over again in different words, they obviously thought I was stupid. 'Did you know your husband had another wife?' 'Did you know your husband was cheating on you?' 'Did you suspect he had another family?' The same questions, over and over. Detective Crowley kept trying to make eye contact with me to help me keep my cool, but honestly, after about ten rounds of the same questions I was tempted just to give them what they wanted and tell them that, yes, I absolutely knew my husband was a bigamist."

Ettie patted her daughter on the shoulder. "Well, it's over now. You're here, and you're safe. Now, drink your tea and try to relax."

Myra was pleased she had gone to her mother. Her mother and her aunt had not spoken of God or preached to her once the whole time she had been there. If they had, Myra was sure she would not have stayed. Myra sipped her tea slowly; her insides were buzzing ready to snap. "The worst part is there's a child involved." Myra glanced at her mom as she spoke.

"A child?"

"Yes. I think Crowley mentioned it to everyone the other night. It wasn't Preston's child, but he must have raised this woman's child. And the child, well he's an adult now, but the child took his last name." Myra wiped away a tear. "I wanted Peter to adopt since it was too late for me to have our own children, but he wouldn't hear of it. I guess my lying, cheating husband married this other woman fifteen years ago, and she had a child at the time from another relationship. So, my husband raised a child with another woman. He had always told me he wasn't interested in children and never wanted to be a father. Guess he lied about that, too!" Myra placed her mug down on the table and rose from her seat. "I need fresh air."

"Where are you going? You can't leave, not in this condition. You're too upset!" Ettie rose too, placing a hand on Myra's shoulder to encourage her to stay.

"I need some air. I just have to go," Myra said as she brushed her mom's hand aside and started for the door.

"Will you be going to the funeral?" Elsa-May asked.

Myra stopped short of leaving the room. She hadn't thought of that. Should she go? Was it the right thing to do? "No, I don't think I can, Aunt Elsa-May. The 'other woman' generally isn't welcome at such events."

Myra took a deep breath, sad that she wasn't even involved in the planning of her own husband's funeral.

* * *

Days later, Myra's resolve to not attend the funeral was still intact. The more she'd thought about it the more she knew it could get ugly. She was pretty sure she had no reason to go anyway. If funerals were supposed to be for paying your last respects to the deceased, she couldn't think of any appropriate last respects she could pay to her husband. Spitting on his grave and screaming at him in his coffin would probably land her in jail for disturbing the peace. No, there was no way she would go to that funeral. Her cell phone rang, and she answered it to hear Detective Crowley's voice.

"I just wanted to check in on you, Myra," he said. "How are you holding up?"

"Oh, I think I'm okay. The police really rattled me, and I'm trying to come to terms with the fact that my husband lied to me since the day he met me."

"I wish you hadn't had to deal with that, but it's over now."

"I can't stop thinking about how in the dark I've been about my husband. How could I have not known he had another family?"

"It must be awful," he said.

"I guess I never thought it strange that we didn't ever see any of his relatives or friends," Myra said.

"He must've worked hard to keep you in the dark, which is pretty typical for someone who's hiding a big secret. Don't beat yourself up."

Detective Crowley's voice was all comfort, no judgment. Myra liked that, needed that.

"And yet," he continued, "I think there's a part of the story that is missing here. What did he tell his family and friends about his married life? I was thinking…"

"Yes, what were you thinking?" Myra pressed.

"Well, I was just wondering if you'd mind if I went to his funeral. I could find some leads."

"I won't be going, of course. I don't think his other family would be happy to see me. I've decided it's best that I don't go. I'm not even involved in anything to do with the funeral. His other family is making all the arrangements; his legal family that is."

"All the more reason for me to go. Sometimes you can learn a lot about a person by going to their funeral."

"Thank you, Ronald. I appreciate everything you're doing."

Chapter 8

Yea, though I walk through the valley of the
shadow of death,
I will fear no evil: for thou art with me;
thy rod and thy staff they comfort me.
Psalm 23:4

Detective Crowley pulled his car into the lot and sat in his car watching the crowd. Getting a feel for a place and sensing the vibe and energy is something he'd learned early on in his detective work. Being a good detective is one part evidence and two parts gut. 'You've got to use all of your senses, or you'll miss something,' his mentor had told him once, years ago. Following that advice had always worked for him.

The first thing he noticed was that the sun was shining. This was strange because in all his years he'd never been to a funeral where the sun was shining. No matter what the day before had looked like weather-wise, and no matter what the skies did the following day, Mother Nature had a way of always making sure it rained and was gray during funerals, but not today. The short sleeves of the mourners and the lack of bobbing black umbrellas sheltering mourners from the sky's tears were noticeable and odd.

Knowing what he knew about Preston Judge, he wasn't surprised in the least. *It's almost like the world has rid itself of a creep,* he thought, *and the weather is helping us celebrate.*

Making his way through the people, he aimed for the graveside funeral tent and took a seat behind the first row, which would be reserved for family. After a few short moments, the grieving family arrived. He saw Mrs. Judge right away and studied her face from behind his sunglasses. She looked sincere in her mourning; he didn't get any impression that her tears were anything but legitimate. He was glad that Mrs. Judge hadn't seen him.

Mrs. Judge was sitting in her chair sniffling and he noticed a long, lean arm was wrapped loosely about her shoulders. His gaze traveled up the arm to the face of the person to whom it belonged. Short, brown spiky hair at the top gave way to the adolescent pimply skin of a young adult. There were no tears sliding out of the eyes of the youth, no puckered frown to indicate mourning, just an arrogant young man's face. *Must be the son,* the detective thought. He made a mental note to check him out.

The sermon was long and Crowley cursed the glare of the sunshine because everyone kept their sunglasses on. It was hard to read people when he couldn't see their eyes. Picking out any suspicious, nervous glances would be difficult, and he wished that it had rained. Mrs. Judge sniffled the entire time and her son dutifully handed her tissue after tissue, keeping one arm about her shoulders.

When the crowd thinned out and the creaking of the pulley could be heard lowering Preston's casket, the detective stood and looked at the mourners. It was a crowd of around eighty people or so, and it was difficult to tell who everyone was. The detective wondered if he'd wasted his time coming to such a well-attended funeral. He suspected there would not be an opening in this crowd for him to mill around and talk to people about who Preston had been.

He returned to his car and called into the police station. From his car, he had a good view of the people at the funeral.

"Maddy? Crowley here. Could you run a check on one Oscar Judge?" He paused, listening to the voice on the other end of the call.

"Sure, do you want to hold?"

"Call me back." He ended the call and waited. Any information Maddy could find out about Preston's stepson might prove useful. The young man had been surprisingly stalwart during the funeral. Perhaps that could have been his way of taking care of his mother.

While he waited for the call back, he watched people. The obligatory clergyman was making his way through the crowd, offering quiet words and a handshakes to all those in attendance. Mrs. Judge stood with her back to his car and dabbed her eyes every few minutes, holding onto the arm of her son as if it were a life raft. No one stood by her side except her son, and in a short space of time the crowd had dispersed.

At other funerals Crowley had been to, he had observed that the family of the deceased stood together in solidarity, as if being shoulder-to-shoulder will keep them upright and supported as they move into the unknown of a future without their loved one. But not at this funeral. If he were a betting man, he'd guess that the deceased's wife and stepson were the only family in attendance; everyone else was just an acquaintance and probably only a casual one at that. Except for Mrs. Judge, the severe lack of nose-blowing and red eyes and the overabundance of sunshine made this scene look more like a 4th of July picnic and less of a funeral. He was about to pull his car out of the parking lot when his cell phone rang. "Hi, Maddy. What have you got for me?"

"There are a few things here. There was an arrest, but charges were dropped. I'll print everything out for you and put it on your desk."

"Good. I'll come look at everything myself later this afternoon. Who laid the charges?"

"Preston Judge. Would that be his father?"

"Stepfather."

Maddy continued, "Shall I run through everything quickly?"

Crowley breathed out heavily. "Go ahead."

"We've got several complaints about the Judges from their neighbors; about one every other month. Patrol officers were called to investigate yelling and shouting coming from the Judge house just two weeks ago."

Crowley immediately thought of Myra. Since Oscar had taken Preston's last name, had Preston adopted him when he married his mother? "Poor girl," he said aloud thinking of Myra. Myra had shared with him how Peter had refused adoption.

"Poor girl?" questioned Maddy. "No, Detective, these reports aren't about a girl, they're about two men. Sounds like Mr. Judge and the man's stepson were arguing and fighting loudly, repeatedly, and that's why the neighbors called to complain. No, I see nothing about a girl or a woman. And Mr. Judge filed a complaint and had his son arrested for stealing his car at one point."

"That is interesting." Crowley was already deep in thought, mulling through the possible implications of the information.

"Is that all then, Detective?" Maddy broke his thoughts.

"Yes. Um, no. Could you take a quick look and tell me if there's anything in the recent reports to explain what the two men were fighting about?"

"Sure, I can do that. Hold a moment."

In less than a minute, she was back on the line. "Okay, says here that two weeks ago an officer came out to the house, called there by the neighbors to confront the two men. They were out on the lawn shouting at each other at 2 a.m. The responding officer, badge #231, made this note on the report:"

'As I left the patrol car and approached the two men on the lawn, I overheard the younger man say to the older, '*You'd better watch your back, I could kill you right now. And I just might!*' Both men stopped talking when I approached them.'

"That's the end of the report," Maddy said.

"There's no more?" Crowley asked.

"Nope. That's the end of it."

Crowley ended the call wondering about the results of the police interview with Oscar. There was evidence on record of him threatening to kill his stepfather, so maybe his interview had turned up some interesting facts.

Chapter 9

A new commandment I give unto you,
That ye love one another;
as I have loved you,
that ye also love one another.
John 13:34

The day of the funeral Myra had stayed behind, honoring her commitment not to attend. She'd applauded herself at first, that morning, proud of her resolve to stand up for what was best for her. Now that she was away from Peter, she realized that what she had seen as a comfortable relationship was something quite the contrary. The controlling relationship had turned her into an introvert when she was once outgoing and energetic.

She couldn't even mourn her husband properly; it was hard to mourn someone who never existed. As she moved from the bathroom to the kitchen, from the kitchen to the living room, from the living room to the living room window that looked out on the yard, she felt unsettled. Her pride in making her own decision about not attending the funeral kept unraveling; she wavered between feeling proud of herself and struggling with grief.

Regardless of how he treated me, regardless of what a sham our marriage was, he was my husband. I took it seriously and gave the best years of my life to that man. Perhaps I should be there to say goodbye, to give myself some closure and allow myself to move on, she thought.

Back and forth, back and forth, her mind led her through a whirlwind of emotions. In one breath she missed him, wishing their marriage had been different, wondering what more she could have done to salvage it, or give it a different outcome. In the next, she was angry, at herself, at him, at the other woman who had wedged herself between her and her husband's chance at happiness. Then she was back to being sad again, recalling how much grief she'd suffered because of the man's lies. And the very next second, she was angry again and wished she had grabbed her courage and used it wisely.

She looked at her watch. *Too late, the funeral is probably over now.* She made herself a cup of tea and walked back to the couch when there was a knock at her door.

Not expecting any visitors, she peered through the window to see who it might be, deciding that if it was someone she didn't know she would just ignore it and get back to her roller coaster of emotions. But the person outside the door struck her in such a way that curiosity got the better of her. Before she even second-guessed her instincts, Myra opened the door to the woman who was dressed in black and standing on her mother's doorstep.

"I'm not surprised you weren't there. I didn't expect a conniving home-wrecker would have the guts to face the rest of us who truly loved him." Her words were spoken with such venom that Myra stepped backwards as if she'd been struck.

Gathering her wits about her, she replied, "You must be Mrs. Judge?"

The woman nodded.

"How did you find me?" Myra asked.

"I saw this address on the notes of one of the officers." She stepped back and looked up at the house. "I see Preston lowered his standards with you and this house." Mrs. Judge laughed. "Right slap in the middle of Amish country, but I can see you have none of those standards." She tilted her chin upwards.

Myra opened her mouth to correct her and inform her that it was her mother's house not the house she once shared with her husband, but stopped herself. The woman was obviously angry, but the same man too had duped her. "I wonder if you might like to come in. I could make you some tea. I'm sure it's been a dreadful day for you and perhaps some tea would help." Words had flown nervously out of Myra's mouth faster than her brain could function.

"I don't want your tea, I don't want to come into your detestable, awful small house. I just came to tell you one thing." The words were spat at Myra with all the hatred and cruelty of a pit viper.

"Oh," Myra said.

"You think you're so sweet, don't you? So innocent. Invite the widow in for tea and try to be my friend. You've messed with the wrong lady, missy. I know what you did and now I'll make you pay for it, to the fullest extent of the law."

"I've done nothing to you. I didn't even know you existed until just recently. What is it you think I've done?"

"Besides stealing my husband? Besides possibly killing my husband? I'll tell you I know that you stole money from me. I know you made Preston do it; you twisted him around your little finger somehow and convinced him to steal from me. I've got an auditor coming in to go over the books of my husband's business." And with that, the woman turned and stomped away, punching angry holes in Ettie and Elsa-May's grass with her stiletto heels.

Myra felt as though she'd been slapped. Taking a seat on the couch, she thought through what the woman had accused her of. Though it had never raised a red flag before, she recalled how her husband had bought their large house and put it in her name. In fact, all of their accounts had been in her name. He'd said that it was for tax purposes and she had taken his word for it.

Another knock at the door jolted her out of her thoughts and she physically braced herself. *If that's her again, I'm not answering the door*, she thought. She was relieved to see Crowley on her doorstep. She let him into the house and Myra immediately spilled the events of the last few moments, barely stopping to take a breath.

"Myra, I think it's time that you get a lawyer. Preston and his wife were wealthy and Preston might have siphoned money to you."

Myra nodded. "I had no idea of anything." She noticed Crowley's formal, dark suit. "You went to the funeral?"

He nodded. "It was a little bizarre, I guess you could say. I made an interesting discovery though."

"Oh, and what's that?" she asked.

"The stepson, Oscar Judge. He and his stepfather didn't get along. In fact, I think there might be more to their story. I'm looking at him as a person of interest. I'll let you know what I find out. I need to go; I just wanted to check and make sure you're okay." They both stood, Crowley gave Myra's arm a squeeze and smiled at her. He walked to the door, looked over his shoulder, and said, "Get a lawyer."

"I hadn't intended to eavesdrop, dear, but I couldn't help but hear all the loud voices at the door from that woman and from the detective." Myra glanced behind her to see her mother standing with arms crossed and an 'I'm your mother, listen to me' look on her face.

"*Mamm*, I didn't know you were home."

"Elsa-May went out by herself. I stayed and had a rest in my room."

"*Mamm*, stuff's getting crazy with all this. I just don't even know what to do next." Myra suddenly felt like she was in the midst of a plot from a bizarre movie.

"I have some ideas. I think this Mrs. Judge is someone we should learn more about, especially because she's threatened you. I wouldn't be surprised if she killed him, especially if money is involved in all of this somehow," Ettie said.

"I don't know. She seems a little erratic right now. Maybe we should keep our distance. She might be crazy and I wouldn't blame her if she is; I know how she must be feeling."

"Well, I've been talking to your aunt and we think it wouldn't hurt if we just spent a little time casing out the house. I can't just sit around and wait for the answer to land on me. I need to be doing something and helping you somehow."

"What house?" Myra asked.

"The Judge house. You know, just see what we can see. Of course, we'll turn over anything interesting we see to the authorities, but it wouldn't hurt to watch for a while to see what happens."

An hour later, Elsa-May came home and helped Ettie convince Myra to drive her and Ettie to the Judge house. Being Amish, the two elderly ladies couldn't drive and Myra had been coerced into driving them.

* * *

104

Myra and the two elderly widows sat hunched down in Myra's car, watching the Judge house. As they waited for something to happen, they whispered amongst themselves, speculating as to the role Preston's first wife might have played in his death.

"I think she found out her money was missing and blamed him and knocked him off," Elsa-May said.

"Hush," Ettie said. "Someone's going up to the house. The woman is answering the door. He's going inside! Are you getting pictures of all this, Myra?"

Myra snapped her camera lens as quickly as she could.

Fifteen minutes later, the man left the house and Myra snapped more photos.

After about an hour of no additional action, Aunt Elsa-May complained of being hungry, so they called it a day.

Later that night, Myra loaded her photos to Google-Images and ran a face match. Stunned with disbelief, she picked up the phone and called Crowley.

* * *

"Crowley speaking."

"Detective, you're not going to believe what we just found. Oh, it's Myra here."

"Yes, I know your voice. What did you find?" Crowley asked.

"I have pictures to prove it. Manuel Garcia was at the Judge house today."

"The Manuel Garcia?"

"Yes."

"Come by the office tomorrow and bring the photos with you. I've also got a few things I'd like to go over with you."

"Sure, about what time?" Myra asked.

"Whenever you can make it here. I'll be going over case files for most of the day, so I should be here unless I get called out," Crowley said.

"Great. I'll try to be there first thing tomorrow,

if that's okay."

"I'll see you then." With that, the conversation ended and Crowley slid his cell phone onto his desk. Dropping his head to his hand, he thought about this entire mess and what it could mean for Myra. The detective normally felt a certain amount of sympathy for victims, but this time it was someone who had been special to him.

The detectives at Randallston either weren't doing their job properly, or were too intimidated to investigate the fact that someone in the Judge household knows Manuel Garcia, a prominent figure in organized crime.

Crowley picked up his phone and called Detective Jenkins. Jenkins informed him that Manuel Garcia was Priscilla Judge's brother. Jenkins did not think that Manuel Garcia had anything to do with his brother-in-law's murder and refused to look into things further.

Chapter 10

*Yea, though I walk through the valley of the
shadow of death,
I will fear no evil: for thou art with me;
thy rod and thy staff they comfort me.*
Psalm 23:4

The next morning, Crowley waited for Myra but she didn't show. When he finally called her cell she told him she'd be in later that day. She offered him no excuse for her lateness and he thought it odd.

Later in the day, just as the detective was considering calling Myra again, a loud knock crashed on the door of his office. Startled, he said, "Come in." The door flung open to reveal Myra standing in the doorway, looking as beautiful as ever. "Have a seat, Myra," he said with a smile.

She closed the door and sat opposite him. Without saying a word, she showed him her camera and clicked through the images of the man coming out of Mrs. Judge's house. Crowley leaned over to get a better look.

Pointing to a clear-shot image of the man who looked like Manuel Garcia, entering the house, Detective Crowley glanced up at Myra. "This is the man you saw?"

She nodded.

"You're right about him being Manuel Garcia. I phoned Detective Jenkins and found out that Priscilla Judge is Manuel Garcia's sister."

Myra looked exhausted, but she didn't let that hold back a weary smile. "Thank you, Crowley. This has all been so emotionally draining. Sometimes I wonder if I will be able to keep myself together much longer."

With sincerity he said softly, "Myra, you are a very strong woman. You'll be okay, because I'll make sure you are. I know none of this makes any sense yet, but I promise you, I'll get to the bottom of this case and find out what happened to Peter."

"You mean Preston?"

Desperation clutched at his chest. "Maybe he

was trying to leave his old life behind. Just because he changed his name doesn't mean he didn't love you. It doesn't mean he wasn't real when he was with you."

A smile tugged at the corners of Myra's lips. "Thank you, Ronald. Well, I should head back. I think Mom's making her famous meatloaf for dinner."

"I haven't had one of Ettie's home-cooked meals in a long time."

Smiling sweetly, Myra made her way toward the door. "Maybe one of these days I can get her to make you one."

"I'll hold you to your word," he replied as she disappeared behind the closing door. He'd been so preoccupied when he heard the name 'Manuel Garcia' that he hadn't reprimanded Myra for poking her nose into things. He was sure Ettie and Elsa-May had something to do with her actions. They must have been at the Judge house spying.

Crowley remained at his desk, sifting through files and documents, trying to figure out who had the best motive for killing Preston Judge. The case was certainly perplexing, but he knew the answer had to be staring him right in the face. The vibration of his cell phone dancing atop his desk jolted him from his thoughts.

"Hello?"

"Crowley? I'm so sorry to call you, but I really have nobody else to ask right now."

"Myra? Is something wrong?" Crowley sprang to his feet and reached for his car keys.

"Well, it's nothing too serious, but my car just stalled out on me. It's been like twenty minutes since I left your office? I was having some problems and figured I just needed gas, but it's still acting up. I turned into a little convenience store just as the car died. I'm sitting there now. I don't know what to do or how to get home."

"I was just about to call it a day and head home myself. I'll come and get you."

"I'm sorry for bothering you. You've saved me again."

"Sit tight, and I'll be there as quick as I can."

"Thank you."

After he jotted down the address, Crowley ended the call and tossed his phone into his pocket. Gathering his belongings, he locked his office and headed to save the damsel in distress.

* * *

After collecting Myra, Crowley had her car towed to a nearby mechanic to have it repaired. The dirty, rumpled old man told them that the alternator looked like it would need to be replaced, and that the car would be ready the next day. They got back into Crowley's car and headed toward Ettie's house.

"You saved the day yet again," Myra commented as they drove.

"I wouldn't say that," Crowley said with laughter. He glanced at Myra and saw that she was deep in thought.

After a few moments of silence, Myra said, "I'm sorry I didn't make it in earlier today. I just couldn't face all of it. I want to wake up and find it's all been a dream."

"That's understandable."

"Why have you always been there for me like you have? It's been years since we were close, yet you still jump at the chance to be there for me; even in the worst of times."

"That's what men do, Myra. Real men are always there for those who matter to them."

Myra scoffed. "Well, there must not be all that many real men out there in the world then."

"It's just a harsh world we live in. Most people start out good-natured with a strong moral code, but environment, loss, and hardships can make even the most pious man a broken husk of his former self." Crowley took his eyes off the road for a brief second to see Myra's reaction. She looked as if she were enveloped in compassion.

"You must be a special person then, considering you were able to keep those traits well into your - your fifties?"

Crowley gave a gruff chuckle. "I just have

impenetrable armour. If I let anything eat away at my defences I'd be just as gone as the rest of them."

"Well, since no woman has ever really gotten into your heart, I suppose that's pretty accurate," she said.

A half smile decorated Crowley's face, but he did his best to hide it from his passenger. One girl had almost cracked his armour, and he was looking at her out of the corner of his eye. "Do you remember that time when we got lost hiking in the woods? I still can't believe I actually talked you into going with me." The thought of this memory caused fuzziness to whirl around in his stomach.

"Oh my gosh, that was such a nightmare! I mean, it was fun looking back at it, but I was terrified. You'd think a cop would know how to use a compass or follow the sun or something!"

Crowley laughed heartily. "Cops don't really get lost all that often, sorry. Remember that spider that crawled in your hair when we were trying to figure out where we were on the map? That was great."

"You jerk! I have never seen such a big, ugly, hairy thing in all my life."

"I must at least get second place then," he said jokingly.

"Oh, please. You might be big and hairy, but you're far from ugly."

Crowley tried to hold back his embarrassment, and hoped she wouldn't interpret his silence as a bad thing.

"You know, sometimes I wonder why we drifted so far apart. I miss having you as a close friend," Myra said.

The sincerity in Myra's voice tugged at the detective's heart. "I miss it too, but life moved on at a fast pace, and we ended up taking different paths. Work took priority, and the next time I heard from you, you didn't seem interested, and that was that."

"We could have been friends."

He had wanted more than that, but he always knew deep down that she deserved so much better than he could ever be. "I just fell so far into my work that I had no time for anything else."

"Right," she replied. "Life has a way of pulling us up and showing us our mistakes."

Crowley paused for a moment and thought about what she'd just said. He had never been one to believe in fate or destiny, but for the first time he had reason to question whether such a thing could exist. Why else would he be sitting next to the only woman he ever regretted not getting to know better? Something brought them together, and he knew he wanted to make the most of it. Without saying it aloud, Crowley vowed that he would solve this case and learn the truth.

Pulling into Ettie's driveway, Crowley offered to walk Myra to the door. "Oh, you don't have to do that."

"I know, but I don't mind. You can't exactly turn down a free police escort now, can you?" he said with a wide grin.

"I suppose I can't." They walked up to the door and said their goodbyes. Suddenly, the door flew open and Ettie stood in front of them.

The smell of meatloaf wafted under Crowley's nose and his mouth watered.

Ettie folded her arms and glared at the two of them. "It's about time you got home. Where have you been? Dinner's getting cold."

"I'm sorry, *Mamm,* but my car broke down and the detective picked me up, had my car towed to the shop, and we just got here now. It's been a long day."

Ettie smiled. "Well, since you're here, Crowley, how about you stay for dinner?"

It was an offer he couldn't refuse.

* * *

Crowley arrived at Ettie's doorstep mid-afternoon the next day. The loud knock had scared the old woman since she wasn't expecting any visitors. Myra came running out of the living room to answer the door.

"I'm sorry, *Mamm.* I forgot to tell you that Crowley called earlier today. He wants to discuss the case with us. He wants your input."

Ettie said, "I should become a private investigator."

Myra giggled and opened the door, revealing the patiently waiting detective.

"Good day, Myra," he said, taking off his hat. She motioned for him to come in, and then the three sat at the kitchen table to discuss the case.

Always accustomed to serving snacks and drinks, Ettie rose to her feet. "Would either of you like some freshly baked cookies or perhaps some tea?"

"No thank you, Ettie. I appreciate the offer though," Crowley said.

Myra shook her head.

Ettie poured herself a cup of tea and sat down to see the detective sprawling several sheets of paper on the table. He slid three photographs in front of the women. "This one is Mrs. Judge, this one is her son," and pointing the last image, "And this is a mug shot of Manuel Garcia; the man whom you both saw visiting the wife."

"And who is that man?" Ettie asked, pointing to a picture that was still halfway inside the folder that housed all of the detective's documents.

"*Mamm*, that's Peter, or Preston I should say. Although, it doesn't look much like him, it must have been when he was a lot younger." Myra took a sideways glance at her mother, ashamed of the silly rift that had kept them apart all those years.

"I'm afraid the Randallston detectives weren't interested in the fact that Manuel Garcia is Priscilla Judge's brother. They said that there's no reason to suspect he had anything to do with Preston's death."

"Do you think revenge would be a solid motive in this case, Crowley? If Preston's wife was brazen enough to show up at my house to threaten my daughter with a lawsuit, who says she isn't capable of having her mobster brother take care of the man who was stealing money from her? She might have found out about the bigamy too."

Crowley nodded. "It's definitely possible. Revenge is a motive, but I couldn't persuade the police in charge of the investigation to see it that way."

Ettie smiled and tried to think of the list of suspects so far. She pulled out a little notebook and went over her scribbles. "Okay, so we have the wife, the stepson, and the wife's brother. Is there anyone else on your radar, Detective?"

"Not currently. It's looking like it was done by someone close to him, which means those three are our prime suspects. I'm just not sure which one I lean toward the most." His face looked grim for a moment.

Myra chimed in, "I think that no matter who actually did it, the wife was probably the mastermind. When she came here to talk to me, I could sense the evil in her."

"Yes, I think that's probably the case," Crowley said. "I'm still leaning toward the son as the one that pulled the trigger, though."

"Trigger?" Myra asked. "I thought he was stabbed."

Crowley chuckled. "I'm sorry, police slang. I just

meant that I think that he is the one who actually committed the murder."

"Oh," she replied.

Still looking at the pictures on the table, Ettie said, "Preston looks very big in that picture. The son is small from these pictures." She tapped on a photo of Oscar Judge. "It'd be like a David and Goliath type of battle if one ever attacked the other, don't you think?"

The detective grew silent for a few minutes. "Hmm, I actually didn't even think about that. That is definitely a great observation, Ettie, but he was stabbed in the back. He might not have seen the person coming since there was no sign of a struggle."

Myra's phone vibrated in her pocket. She pulled the phone and looked at it. "Oh, it's the repair shop. One second." Ettie and Crowley sat quietly as the conversation played out. Once the call had ended, Myra said, "The car is ready to be picked up."

"Wonderful. I'll take you there now," Crowley said.

Interrupting the two, Ettie questioned the detective, "Would you like to stay for dinner again? Surely the car can wait until afterwards." The look that both her daughter and Crowley gave her, soured her enthusiasm.

"I'm sorry, Ettie, but I'll have to take a rain check," Crowley said.

"Yeah, *Mamm.* The mechanic said they close at five and it's already a little after four o'clock."

Smiling, Crowley nodded before throwing on his hat and coat and following Myra to his car.

Chapter 11

And let us not be weary in well doing:
for in due season we shall reap, if we faint not.
Galatians 6:9

Detective Crowley and Myra pulled into the parking lot of the repair shop to see Myra's car sitting in front of the garage.

The same mechanic that they had left the car with greeted them. "She's running like new," he said. Dirt was smeared across the mechanic's aging face. "It's gonna run you about five fifty though."

Myra handed over her credit card. They followed the mechanic through to the corner of the workshop which he used as his office. He ran it through the machine, but it was rejected.

"Try it again," Myra insisted.

The mechanic ran it through his machine once more. "Nope." He picked up the printed ticket. "Says 'insufficient funds.'"

Myra pulled a face. "That can't be right."

Grabbing his wallet without hesitation, Crowley pulled the mechanic aside and paid the invoice. He looked back to see Myra staring at him with confusion. He took his receipt and walked back toward her. Throwing her the keys, he smiled.

"What did you do?" Myra asked.

"Here's your receipt," he said, handing it to her. "Just in case you have any problems and need to come back."

She smiled sweetly. "Thank you. I'll pay you back just as soon as I can get to the bank. I can't understand what's happened to my credit card."

"No hurry. I'll go to the station and go over the evidence again. If you or your mother needs anything at all, please call me right away."

"Of course," Myra replied as Crowley opened the door and got into his car.

"Crowley."

"Yes?"

"Thank you again for everything. You've been a rock during the most difficult time of my life. I can't thank you enough for that."

He noticed her right hand was over her heart. He smiled. "Anytime."

* * *

Back at his office, Detective Crowley combed through evidence. He had taken over Peter Davis's Missing Persons case from the Lancaster police and had the file in front of him. Despite what Myra had told him, Crowley could see that the police had been quite thorough in their investigations. They had gone over the house for prints, but he wondered how they could have missed the golf club—and, even more, the toothbrush. Peter had no cell phone and no credit cards registered in his name. The local police had patrol cars looking for Peter's missing car.

As he threw ideas around in his mind, he realized he was missing a key piece of evidence: the stepson's interrogation. Surely the investigating detectives would have taped the session and they still hadn't supplied him with the tapes of Mrs.

Judge's questioning as they had promised. He picked up his cell and rang the detective from Randallston.

"Hello? It's Detective Crowley. I'm calling about the Preston Judge case."

"How can I help you, Detective?" Detective Jenkins sounded as though he was bored.

"You still haven't sent me the tapes of Mrs. Judge's questioning and I was hoping to also get a hold of the tape of Oscar Judge's interview. Could I get a copy of them tomorrow? I'll have one of my officers drive there and pick them up."

"There are no tapes, Detective. We haven't conducted any such interviews with them outside of a few unrecorded questions at the victim's home."

Crowley tapped the pencil in his hand loudly on his desk.

Jenkins continued, "We're treating this as a random killing."

"Are you serious? The victim was a bigamist living a double life; Mrs. Judge thinks he drained money from her and put it into his other wife's name. I already know that the stepson had threatened to kill him, and the wife's brother is in organized crime. How are you not looking into any of them?"

"Firstly, there is no evidence to suggest that anyone close to the victim is at fault for this crime. Secondly, you're right, this is our case not yours."

"That's insane! Every single strand of evidence points directly to the wife or a member of her family."

"I understand it might be frustrating, Detective, but we just don't have any proof of that. The case will remain open, but we've other cases that need our attention."

"That's bogus."

"I'm in charge of this investigation. If you want me to keep you informed of the case, I'll thank you to leave the running of it up to me."

Crowley knew he'd overstepped the mark. "Yes, of course. I'd appreciate being kept informed on anything that might come to light." Crowley scratched his head in frustration. They had been all over Myra, practically accusing her of being involved in some manner, and not trusting what she told them. But, it appeared Manuel Garcia was being treated as an innocent bystander even though he was a known gangster. "I take it that Myra Davis is no longer on your radar as a suspect then?"

"We didn't really suspect her, we just had to speak with her. It's difficult to accept the fact that she was living with the man for over ten years and never knew about his double life."

"Mrs. Judge didn't know either, did she?"

"She says that she had no idea."

"Yet you don't find it strange that Mrs. Judge didn't suspect a thing? But you do find it strange that Myra didn't?" Crowley sighed in anger.

"Well, that aside. I'm sorry, Detective, I really am. Our hands are bound too. There's just not enough evidence to go on right now. When we get wind of something more substantial, we'll happily take a look into it."

"All right; well, thank you for your time. I'll

investigate from this end and if I find anything else out I'll let you know."

"Please do, Detective Crowley. There is a small lead I'm having one of my men follow up on."

"What's that?" Crowley asked listening carefully. It seemed to Crowley that the Randallston police wanted him to think that they weren't investigating further, but they were if they were still following leads.

Jenkins continued, "It may be nothing, but two weeks before Preston Judge's death, his executive personal assistant, Aiden Addison, quit. It shocked everyone at the firm; he'd been with Preston for over ten years and he offered no reason for quitting. We've been unable to locate Addison."

Crowley ran a hand through his hair. What could a disgruntled employee have to do with the whole mess? "I'll keep in touch," Crowley said before he ended the call. He flung his cell across the room and it bounced off the wall. What was going on? Something wasn't right. He continued sifting through the files on his desk, looking for that one needle in the gigantic haystack. He dropped his head into his hands and let out a deep sigh. This case was too important to let some knuckleheaded investigators mess it up.

He called Myra's cell phone. "Hey, we have a problem."

"Hi, Crowley. What's wrong?"

"It seems the police in Randallston are chalking the homicide up as a random killing. They don't feel there's enough evidence to investigate any of the three suspects we came up with."

The tone of her voice grew darker. "You have got to be kidding me. Maybe they're getting paid off to sweep it under the rug."

"I keep coming back to the brother-in-law, but there's nothing to prove that he was in any way involved."

"He could have bribed someone to keep quiet – maybe bribed the police?"

"I'd hate to think that. We just have to keep our noses to the pavement until we find something solid that can't be argued."

"I understand. Well, thanks for the update, Ronald. I'll let Mom know.

"Thank you," he said as he ended the call.

Looking at his computer screen, the image of Preston Judge was staring back at him. "What am I missing, Mr. Judge? Who did this to you, and why did you drain your accounts and put everything in Myra's name? Help me find justice for you and Myra. Please."

* * *

Ettie was crocheting a rug when Myra walked in, looking upset. "What's wrong, dear? You've slept in and missed breakfast."

"Oh, *Mamm,* missing breakfast is the least of my problems."

"I could fix you some pancakes."

Myra shook her head and sat opposite Ettie. "Crowley called me last night and told me that the Randallston police think Peter was killed by some random person and they aren't continuing with the

133

investigations. They told Crowley that there's no evidence to link any of our three suspects to his death."

Ettie's mouth pinched together. "So there's been no development since the last time Crowley was here?"

Myra shook her head.

"There's more than enough probable cause to at least consider the wife, the brother-in-law and particularly the stepson. The stepson even threatened him," Ettie said.

"They won't even bring them in for questioning. It doesn't make any sense to me, but I don't know much about police procedures. Without concrete proof they won't go further."

Ettie's face grew stern. "Well, if they won't do their job, we'll just have to do it for them."

Myra scrunched her eyebrows and studied Ettie. "What do you mean, *Mamm*?"

"Her son. What do we know about the little deviant? Let's look over what we know, and then I think we should watch him."

This caught Myra off guard. "*Mamm*, we can't just keep going around following and recording these people. What if they catch us? Have you ever heard of 'the mob'?"

"Mob of what? What mob?"

Myra rolled her eyes. "The Mob is a criminal organization – the worst, everyone is afraid of them."

"*Fear not for I am with you,* the Scripture says. If you're scared, you can stay behind. Elsa-May will come with me."

A loud sigh escaped Myra's lungs. "I just don't think it's a smart idea. Let Crowley do that. I'm sure he won't mind if we just call and ask him."

Ettie shook her head. "*Nee*, let him do his thing. I'm sure he already has his own ideas of how to make some progress in this case. He's helped us enough. Now it's our turn to do a little footwork."

Myra reluctantly agreed.

They gathered at the table where Crowley had sat with them the day before. Myra scattered some pictures and notes across the surface and the two women dived into the maze of confusion and evidence.

"We know that his name is Oscar Judge. He's twenty years old and isn't Preston Judge's biological son. According to the paperwork that Crowley provided, he's been in and out of their home since he was young. He stayed with his biological father at times when things at the Judge home were unpleasant." Ettie breathed out noisily. "There are several 911 calls on record showing that arguments and domestic violence were common in the household whenever the son was in the home. We know he stole Preston's car, but the charges were dropped for some reason."

Ettie shuffled around some of the papers and dove into deep thought. "There were several emergency calls about noise disturbances at the house, but the boy was never charged with any of those. One time an officer heard the boy threatening the stepfather."

"Oscar's record is clean apart from the car incident according to Crowley." Myra read from a sheet of paper. "According to this, the stepson is currently working odd jobs here and there. He has never held long-term employment."

"Do we know where this boy has been living recently?"

"Crowley thinks he's staying with his mother while he's in town. He just came down to attend the funeral apparently," Myra said.

"It looks like we're heading back there then." Ettie was insistent as usual.

"To the Judge house?" Myra asked.

Ettie nodded.

"All right, *Mamm*. We can watch him from a distance for a while. If he really is involved in this, he's far too dangerous for two women to be messing with on their own."

"I understand, Myra; I really do. I just can't let this go unsolved. There are too many unanswered questions hanging around in the air. Like, why would Peter put everything in your name unless he felt something bad would happen to him?"

Myra pondered the thought for a moment.

"That's a good point, actually. Maybe I should run that by Crowley before we go."

Ettie shook her head in disagreement. "*Nee.* Let's just try. If we don't get something after a few hours, we can do it your way and go through Crowley."

A loud knock on the door startled them both. Ettie opened the door to see the mailman.

"I've got a registered letter that needs to be signed for."

"Who is it for?" Ettie asked the mailman.

"Myra Davis."

"Myra?" Ettie called out.

Myra stepped forward. "I had my mail redirected." She signed for the letter. When the mailman left, she took the letter. All strength left her when she saw the handwriting. "*Mamm*, it's a letter from Peter; it's his handwriting."

Ettie drew her eyebrows together. "Quick, open it."

Myra ripped open the envelope and read:

Myra,

If you get this letter it means that something bad has happened to me. I've instructed the lawyers to send this letter to you. If I am dead, I guess you found out the truth about me already.

I want you to know that I was trapped in a web of lies. I wanted to give you the best life possible, but if I left Priscilla I know that they would kill me. I'm sorry I treated you harshly. I know my life would've been easier if you hated me and left me. You were always too good for me and I knew it, but I needed you in my life and couldn't let you go. If only I'd been completely free, then our lives could've been perfect. I would've been free to treat you how you deserved to be treated.

If my plan turns out correctly I should have left you with enough money to keep you comfortable for the rest of your life. I couldn't continue in this charade. Forgive me for what I've done, but I couldn't see a way out of the darkness.

Love Peter.

Myra passed the note to Ettie. "Part of me didn't want to believe that Peter was Preston. Now I know that it must be true."

Ettie read the whole letter and looked up at Myra. "Sounds like a suicide note."

"Do you think so? He says 'forgive him for what he's done.' He would have meant staying married to that other woman."

"I suppose you could read his letter either way," Ettie said

"But he was stabbed in the back—it couldn't have been a suicide. Nothing makes sense."

"Could he have been planning to kill himself and was killed before he could carry out his plan? Is the letter really from him?"

Myra studied the note. "It's his hand writing. And it's something he would have a lawyer do; he was a meticulous planner."

"We'll have to show it to Crowley. It's evidence. It says there that he feared he'd be killed if he left her."

"I'll drive to Crowley's office and show him in

person," Myra said.

"I'll come with you," Ettie said.

When they showed Crowley the letter, he rang and confirmed with Preston Judge's lawyer. The lawyer was instructed to send the letter in the event of Preston's death. Crowley took the letter as evidence and drove to the Randallston police who were handling the murder investigation. Detective Crowley told the ladies he'd meet them at Ettie's house that evening.

Chapter 12

Truly my soul waiteth upon God: from him
cometh my salvation.
He only is my rock and my salvation;
he is my defence; I shall not be greatly moved.
Psalm 62:1

Ettie and Elsa-May invited all the widows to come to the house that evening to hear what Crowley had to say when he came back from Randallston.

Elsa-May walked into the living room from the kitchen holding a large cake. "What we need is cake and *kaffe.*"

"*Gut.* I'll get the *kaffe,* Elsa-May, you cut the cake," Ettie said. When Ettie came back in the room with the coffee, she sat on the couch. "There must be something we're missing."

"The girls are coming tonight for a widows meeting. We can go over all the evidence then," Elsa-May told Myra.

"That's good," Myra said.

The three younger widows, Emma, Maureen, and Silvie breezed through the door. They'd arrived in one buggy. Once they were all brought up to speed with recent events, they expressed their sympathies to Myra.

Myra looked down at her hands.

"He did make sure you were looked after," Elsa-May said.

Myra nodded. "It makes sense now."

"What does?" Ettie frowned.

"Sometimes he used to be so cruel to me, but now I know that he loved me. I wish I'd understood. I wish he'd told me."

Ettie scoffed. "You say that now, but I don't think you'd have taken too kindly to the knowledge of another wife."

Myra sighed.

"From what Ettie told us of his letter, it sounds like he thought his life would be in danger if he left the other marriage," Maureen said.

"That's right," Emma said.

"He was taking money from his wife and giving it to you. Sounds like a reason for the family or someone close to the wife, to have him killed." Emma gave a sharp nod.

"I will give the money back to her," Myra said with tears glistening in her eyes.

"I don't think so." A deep voice sounded from the front door.

All eyes turned to Crowley as he walked into the house. He took a seat on an old wooden chair. Just as he opened his mouth to speak, his cell phone sounded. Pulling it out of his pocket, he said, "Excuse me, ladies."

The ladies fell silent as the detective walked into the kitchen while speaking to someone on his cell phone.

When he finished and came back into the room, Elsa-May asked, "What is it, Detective? Is it something about this case?"

"It seems that Preston's assistant has also gone missing. He quit two weeks before the murder and now they can't locate him. They want to ask him questions about some missing money." A beep sounded on Crowley's phone. "That'll be the photo of the assistant." He looked at the photo and then breathed out heavily. "If you ladies will excuse me, I'll just have to make a quick call."

He stepped out of the room, but the ladies fell silent and listened to the detective. They heard him say, "Jenkins, it appears you've sent me a photo of Preston Judge in error rather than his assistant. What? Are you certain?" Two minutes later, Crowley ended the conversation and walked back into the room and sat down.

"What is it, Detective?" Elsa-May asked. "You look like you've been punched in the stomach."

He leaned over and handed his phone to Myra. "Do you recognize this man?"

Myra took the phone and studied the image on the display. "Of course, that's Peter, well, Preston."

The detective took his cell phone back. "According to the police, that is Aiden Addison, Preston's assistant."

Myra's face scrunched. "What?"

"Myra, how much money is in your bank account, if you don't mind me asking?" the detective asked.

"I don't know exactly to the dollar, but there's over six hundred thousand."

Ettie gasped. "That's a lot of money."

"He said that he inherited $500,000. That's how much he had when we married. The rest, he saved."

"Can you check your account now?" Crowley asked.

Myra nodded. "I've got my laptop in the car."

"Go check it please, Myra," Crowley said.

Myra left to check her bank account while the widows and Crowley talked.

"So they look very similar do they, this Aiden and Preston?"

"Appears so," Crowley said scratching his chin. "And similar to Peter."

"What do you mean? Are these three people all the one person?" Elsa-May asked.

"Who was Myra's husband then?" Emma asked.

Before Crowley could say more, Myra came back into the house. "I'm not able to access my

147

account anymore. It tells me I'm using the wrong password."

The widows gasped.

Ettie rushed to her side. "Sit down. He or someone must have changed the password."

"I'll take you to the bank tomorrow, Myra. No use jumping to conclusions until we know for certain," Crowley said.

Myra nodded. "Now, I'm worried. When my credit card didn't work the other day, I just thought it was a problem at the mechanic's end."

"It's looking like this Aiden character was posing as Peter," Crowley said. "Not only that, he framed Preston to make it look like he was a bigamist."

"Surely you're jumping to too many conclusions," Ettie said.

"But the DNA match, Detective," Maureen said.

Elsa-May said, "I thought it funny that everything was gone except the toothbrush for a convenient DNA match to Preston Judge and the golf club for the fingerprints."

"Peter planted Preston's toothbrush?" Silvie

asked.

"That would fit what has happened," Crowley said.

"So Aiden was posing as Peter, killed Preston and made it look like Preston and Peter were the same person? And then Aiden disappeared?"

"Not only that," Crowley said. "We don't know who Aiden Addison is; he was using the identity of someone who died years ago."

The widows gasped.

"So you're chasing ghosts?" Silvie asked.

"Seems so," Crowley said. "Aiden, or I should say the man posing as Aiden, tried to construct the perfect crime. It seems Preston was never a bigamist. I'd say that Aiden has posed as Peter Davis and had been siphoning money from Preston Judge's company for years."

"Do you think that Aiden killed Preston?" Emma asked.

"There's no proof of that as yet, but it would be difficult to find someone who doesn't exist," Detective Crowley said. "Peter doesn't officially exist, and neither does Aiden."

"You say Aiden Addison was Preston's assistant, then tried to make it look like Preston was a bigamist posing as Peter, and someone murdered Preston?" Maureen asked.

"Seems so." Crowley scratched his head.

"But if Aiden Addison didn't exist, how could Aiden hold down a job if he didn't really exist and didn't have a social security number?" Myra asked.

"According to the Randallston police, he was using the social security information of someone who had died. Government agencies don't routinely cross check social security numbers for death certificates if someone applies for a passport, life insurance or the like. This Aiden fellow was using the identity of someone born in 1919. For some reason, he found it convenient to keep some money in your name, Myra."

Myra rose to her feet. "I'm sorry, I've got a bad headache. I need to go to bed."

Crowley leaped to his feet. "You okay, Myra?"

She shook her head. "I need to sleep." Myra

walked out of the room.

When Myra was out of the room, Silvie said, "I feel sorry for Myra. She just got used to the idea of her husband being Preston Judge, a bigamist, and now no one is quite sure who he was."

"Could he still be alive?" Maureen whispered.

"It seems more than likely that Peter was this Aiden character, and he had this planned for a long time," Crowley said.

"Is that unusual, Detective? This man would have been living a lie for over ten years. If he was posing as Aiden Addison why add another identity, the Peter Davis identity?"

Crowley shook his head. "He could have had several identities. I've read of cases like this one in the Police Journals. Anyway, the Randallston police checked out the residential address Aiden had given his employer and found that it's an abandoned warehouse."

* * *

Crowley was there right at nine o'clock the next morning to take Myra to the bank. Myra checked her account to find that there was no money. Not only was there no money, just over one million dollars had been deposited and withdrawn on the day of Preston Judge's funeral.

Crowley ushered a crying Myra out of the bank. "I thought at least he wanted me to be comfortable, and now I have nothing. He wouldn't let me work, so now I have no job to go to."

Crowley's hand rested on her elbow as they walked. He had no idea what to say to her. "I'm sorry, Myra. I don't know how someone could do this to you. Do you want to go back to your mother's place now?"

Myra took a tissue out of her handbag and dabbed at her eyes. "I want you to find him, Ronald."

"I'll do my best. I'll take you back to your mother's and tell the others working on the case what we've discovered about the money. Is there anything you might be able to tell me about Peter? Anything you can think of that might be relevant?"

Myra rubbed her forehead. "No, I can't think of anything that I haven't already told you."

"You still have the house, don't you?" Crowley asked.

Myra nodded. "I still have my house. I'm glad he didn't touch that."

Crowley took Myra back to Ettie's house. Myra sat around the kitchen table with Crowley, Ettie and Elsa-May.

"Why don't we hatch a plot to trap him? Plant a trap, or whatever the term is," Ettie said.

"I'm listening." Elsa-May leaned toward Ettie.

Ettie's lips turned down. "That's all I've got so far."

Crowley put his hands up. "I do like discussing and brain-storming with you ladies. You do come up with some good ideas, but that's where it must stop." He looked at Ettie. "No plans to trap anyone, please."

Ettie narrowed her eyes at Crowley and pressed her lips together.

Elsa-May sighed. "He must have left a clue

somewhere. Can you think of something he might have said about his past, Myra? A place, a name or anything that might help?"

"I can't think of anything. We don't even know for sure if Peter was Preston or whether he was this Aiden fellow." Myra put her head in her hands. "Why did I get that letter from Preston's lawyer in Peter's handwriting? Nothing makes sense. I need to lie down." Ettie ushered Myra into her bedroom to lie down then Ettie came back to join Elsa-May and the detective.

"Can we trace him through the bank? Would he have gone into the bank, or did he transfer the money electronically?" Elsa-May asked the detective.

"Would he be leaving the country?" Ettie asked.

"The funds were transferred electronically. He might leave the country, or might have already left. There are hundreds of ways he could leave the country and without a name, we're powerless to stop him." Crowley was quiet and rubbed his chin for a moment. "He can change his name, but it's not so easy to change one's personality."

"What are you thinking, Crowley?" Elsa-May asked.

"What were his interests? We might be able to track the man down that way. Maybe he had an unusual hobby?" Crowley raised his eyebrows waiting for a reply.

"I don't know. Myra never mentioned such a thing," Ettie said.

"Well, we have nothing else to go on. I'll ask the police from Randallston what they know about Aiden Addison. If they can't come up with anything, I might have to make another trip to Randallston to see what I can uncover. Maybe I'll should take a look around Myra's house." Crowley rubbed his chin again. "I'm sure Myra holds a clue in her mind somewhere. She must know where he'd go or what he'd do. He couldn't keep his defenses up for ten whole years. He must've let something slip."

* * *

Ettie went to speak to Myra, who was lying on her bed.

"I heard them, *Mamm*. And I can't think of anything; I can't think where he'd be."

Ettie sat on the side of the bed. "Did he ever mention places he'd like to go or places he'd visited?"

Myra sat up. "Make me a cup of tea? I'll think about it while you're gone."

"Okay," Ettie said as she stood up. "Just relax and something will come to you."

"Yeah, no pressure," Myra said under her breath. "*Mamm*, tomorrow I'll go home. I need to sort my life out." Myra was grateful to everyone trying to put the pieces of the puzzle together, but she just wanted to forget everything for just a moment. While she was staying with her mother and her aunt, she knew she wouldn't be able to escape the constant pressure and questions.

Chapter 13

Be strong and of a good courage, fear not,
nor be afraid of them: for the LORD thy God,
he it is that doth go with thee;
he will not fail thee, nor forsake thee.
Deuteronomy 3:16

Myra unlocked her front door and stepped into her house. She knew she would never feel comfortable there again. At least the house was in her name, so she could sell it and buy something smaller. Even though it was comforting to have her mother and Aunt Elsa-May around, Myra was glad to get back to her microwave, air-conditioning and the television. She set her handbag down on the hall-table by the front door and headed to the kitchen to make a cup of coffee.

After she had taken a deep breath of the fresh coffee beans she ground, Myra felt a chill down her back and turned around. Peter stood in front of her. She swallowed hard. "Who are you?"

He frowned at her, and took a step toward her without a hint of expression on his face. "Don't you know your own husband?"

"I thought you were dead."

"That's what I wanted everyone to think. Come away with me, Myra." He took another step toward her and pulled her roughly into his arms.

She sank into his familiar chest for a moment before she pushed him away. "Stop it. Who are you? Preston or Aiden?"

A smirk tickled at his lips. "Ah, I see. They know about Aiden. They're smarter than I gave them credit for."

"Tell me what's going on."

"Do you love me, Myra?"

"I loved Peter, but I don't know who you are anymore. Tell me what's happening?"

"I had to do it for the money, so we could get away from here and be comfortable. I couldn't tell you what I was doing. You would've found some reason to disagree."

Myra rubbed her eyes. "But you don't exist. Peter

Davis doesn't exist. I know your birth certificate's not real. Who are you?"

He smirked. "What does a name matter?"

"It matters to me. I don't know who you are."

"You lived with me for ten years; you know who I am. Come away with me quickly. I've got flights booked for us."

Myra looked down at the ground. "This can't be happening," she murmured. She looked up at Peter. "You wanted me to think you were Preston?"

"Only until I came to get you, and here I am. I do share an uncanny resemblance to Preston. I worked for him for a while, watching his crooked deals, before I decided to get some for myself. His accounting system was horrendous; I saw an opportunity, and I took it."

"Did you kill him?"

"Myra, Myra, Myra. Of course, I had to kill him for my plan to work. I did it for you."

"For me?" Myra fumbled in her pocket to make sure her cell phone was still there. "What was your plan? But first tell me your real name."

"My real name isn't important. I've had so many names I barely remember who I am." Peter laughed.

"Tell me what you did - your plan."

"We don't have much time, I'll tell you on the way to the airport."

Myra walked over to a loveseat in the hallway and sat down. "Tell me."

He sat next to her. "I'll tell you, only if you promise you'll come with me."

Myra nodded. She needed to have him tell her, so she could tell Crowley.

"I was working for Judge a little before I met you at that gallery. I fell in love with you the moment I saw you." He ran his hand over her hair. "You've got the face of an angel and I'm a sucker for a blonde. I knew I was going to take Judge down at some point, so I kept you away from it by taking on a different identity and letting you think that I worked elsewhere."

"So …" Myra sobbed into a tissue she had drawn from her pocket. "You really loved me?"

"Never stopped."

"How did the lawyer send me that letter?" Myra dabbed at her eyes.

"I was Preston's executive assistant. I did everything for him. He asked me to hand deliver documents to his lawyer." He scoffed. "One was a letter to his no good son apologizing for harsh treatment, to be sent to Oscar in the event of Preston's death."

"You read them?"

"Of course, and replaced the letter with a letter to you, from Preston." Peter laughed. "That was the best part of my plan. I came up with a plan so Aiden could disappear and so could Peter Davis. They'd never be able to find Aiden - the real Aiden Addison died years ago, and I had them think that Peter Davis was Preston. I even waited until I was sure the police had searched the house and given up on me before I planted Preston's toothbrush and golf club for you to find."

"Why did you have to involve Peter Davis? Couldn't Aiden have just quit and no one would have ever known about the identity of Peter Davis?"

Peter shook his head. "I had to make it look like Preston was killed by one of his family. He didn't get along with Oscar or his wife. His brother-in-law is a known felon, so the police would have looked in every direction other than Aiden Addison. Do you see?"

"I guess, but why keep up the charade for ten whole years?"

"Three million reasons, Myra. Three million, two hundred, and thirty reasons to be exact. Besides, we had a comfortable life didn't we?" Peter stood and dragged Myra to her feet. "Let's go. I've got a car parked around the corner. There's no need to pack; we can buy everything you need."

Myra pulled away from him. "I'm sorry, Peter, I can't go with you."

Peter's face stiffened. "You said you would go with me if I told you what happened."

She stepped away from him. "I'll give you half an hour to get away before I call the police."

"No, Myra."

Myra took two steps further away. "I can't go with you, Peter. What you did was wrong."

"I can't leave you here to tell the police about me. Surely you can't be that stupid, Myra."

His eyes glistened with evil. Myra turned and ran up the stairs toward her bedroom. She pulled the cell out of her pocket as she ran and pressed Crowley's number on speed dial. Peter lunged for the phone and knocked it out of her hands. Myra got into the bedroom and shut the door, but before she could lock it, he kicked the door open. Screaming, Myra ran into her open closet as he tackled her and knocked her off her feet landing on top of her.

"I'm sorry it had to end this way, but you're mucking up my plan." He put both hands around her neck.

A loud crash came from downstairs. "Police."

Peter sprang to his feet while pulling a small gun from his pocket. He ran from Myra.

"He's got a gun," Myra yelled in fright.

Five gunshots rang out. Myra held her breath unable to move. She closed her eyes hoping someone hadn't just died in her house. Myra heard footsteps up the stairs and they got louder as they came toward her. Was it Peter coming to finish her off? Keeping her eyes tightly shut, she prayed for the first time in years. When she opened her eyes, she saw Crowley standing over her.

"Myra? Are you hurt?"

"I'm all right." She put her hand out to Crowley, and he pulled her up. "Did you shoot him?"

Crowley shook his head. "He got out the back door, but I had two cars follow me here. They'll pick him up."

Myra sank into Crowley's arms and he held her tight as she sobbed. "How did you know he'd be here?"

"Gut instinct. I had a feeling he might reach out to you. Ten years is a long time to be with someone, and if he was as controlling as you say, he wouldn't like to let go of the control that easily."

Myra sobbed.

"You're safe now, Myra. You're safe." Crowley's cell phone buzzed, and he drew it out of his pocket with one hand; the other was holding onto Myra. "Yep?"

"Got him," the voice bellowed from the other end of the phone.

"Good; take him to the station. I'll be right behind you." Crowley pushed the cell phone back into his pocket.

"I don't have to go too, do I?"

"Not today. I'll take you back to your mother's before I head to the station."

On the way back to Ettie's house, Myra told him everything that the man she had known as Peter had told her. "I still don't know his real name. He never told me that."

"I don't think it should matter to you what his real name is. We'll run his fingerprints, but as far as you're concerned, you know he's not a person to be trusted. Over the past years, according to the auditors of Preston Judge's business, three and a half million dollars is unaccounted for."

Myra nodded.

Crowley glanced over at her. "You've been

through some terrible times."

"I thought he was missing, then I was made to believe he was Preston, then found he might still be alive and possibly posing as Aiden." Myra sniffled. "Then he tried to kill me."

"It's amazing what people will do for money. Stay with your mother for a while; then sell the house and make a fresh start."

"I can't stay with my mother for too long. We never see eye to eye on anything."

"I'll take you out for dinner or for the day when things get too bad."

"Would you?"

Crowley glanced over at her and smiled.

Myra knew Crowley was one man she could rely on; he had always been the same. She wondered what the future might hold for the two of them.

For now, she wanted to feel safe back at Ettie and Elsa-May's little old house. The house had no electricity, no television, and she had to sleep on the couch, but it was a house filled with love and safety. It was the same safe feeling that she had gotten after she had prayed for the first time in years. She knew the safe feeling was the peace of God, which passes understanding. She took a deep breath as the same calm and peace filled her entire being.

"You all right, Myra?"

She took a sideways glance at Crowley. "Yes, I am, for the first time in a long time."

* * *

Peter Davis had refused to give his real name when he was arrested two days ago. He had relented one day ago so he could secure a lawyer. Crowley immediately set about to find out as much as he could about the man who had caused Myra so much pain.

The fax machine in Crowley's office made a whirring noise. Since he was about to leave for the day he stood by the fax machine in case it was something important. He picked up the pages and read them as they spilled out of the machine.

Crowley read that Ethan Brown, who had posed as Peter Davis and Aiden Addison, was a fifty eight year old man born in Baltimore. His father was still alive, but hadn't seen Ethan in twenty years. Ethan's two siblings and his mother were deceased. Ethan was trained in accounting and had no prior convictions. Breathing out heavily, Crowley found it hard to believe a man such as he did not have any priors. Now that the department knew his real identity, they had a better chance of tracking down false identities he might have used in the past. Crowley silently vowed he would make it his mission to find out who else this man had conned.

Looking at his watch, Crowley saw that it was nearly six. It would be about dinnertime at Ettie and Elsa-May's house. He was sure that Myra would want to know the real name of the man to whom she had been married. A smile twigged at the corners of his mouth as he swung his trench coat over his shoulders. He would soon see Myra again.

* * * * * * * * * * * * * * * *

Thank you for your interest in
That Which Was Lost

To join Samantha Price's
email list and be kept up to date with
New Releases and Special Offers subscribe at:
www.samanthapriceauthor.com

If you have enjoyed this series you might also
enjoy the new spin-off series
Ettie Smith Amish Mysteries
Book1
Secrets Come Home

After Ettie Smith's friend, Agatha, dies, Ettie is surprised to find that Agatha has left her a house. During building repairs, the body of an Amish man who disappeared forty years earlier is discovered under the floorboards.

When it comes to light that Agatha and the deceased man were once engaged to marry, the police declare Agatha as the murderer. Ettie sets out to prove otherwise. Soon Ettie hears rumors of stolen diamonds, rival criminal gangs, and a supposed witness to the true murderer's confession.

When Ettie discovers a key, she is certain it holds the answers she is looking for.

Will the detective listen to Ettie's theories when he sees that the key belongs to a safe deposit box?

Ettie Smith Amish Mysteries Book 2
<u>Amish Murder</u>

When a former Amish woman, Camille Esh, is murdered, the new detective in town is frustrated that no one in the Amish community will speak to him. The detective reluctantly turns to Ettie Smith for help. Soon after Ettie agrees to see what she can find out, the dead woman's brother, Jacob, is arrested for the murder. To prove Jacob's innocence, Ettie delves into the mysterious and secretive life of Camille Esh, and uncovers one secret after another.

Will Ettie be able to find proof that Jacob is innocent, even though the police have DNA evidence against him, and documentation that proves he's guilty?

Can Ettie uncover the real murderer amongst the many people who had reasons to want Camille dead?

Ettie Smith Amish Mysteries Book 3:
<u>Murder in the Amish Bakery</u>

When Ettie has problems with her bread sinking in the middle, she turns to her friend, Ruth Fuller, who owns the largest Bakery in town.

When Ruth and Ettie discover a dead man in Ruth's Bakery with a knife in his back, Ruth is convinced the man was out to steal her bread recipe.

It was known that the victim, Alan Avery, was one of the three men who were desperate to get their hands on Ruth's bread secrets.

When it's revealed that Avery owed money all over town, the local detective believes he was after the large amount of cash that Ruth banks weekly.

Why was Alan Avery found with a Bible clutched in his hand? And what did it have to do with a man who was pushed down a ravine twenty years earlier?

Ettie Smith Amish Mysteries Book 4
<u>Amish Murder Too Close</u>

Elderly Amish woman, Ettie Smith, finds a body outside her house. Everything Ettie thought she knew about the victim is turned upside down when she learns the dead woman was living a secret life. As the dead woman had been wearing an engagement ring worth close to a million dollars, the police must figure out whether this was a robbery gone wrong. When an Amish man falls under suspicion, Ettie has no choice but to find the real killer.

What information about the victim is Detective Kelly keeping from Ettie?

When every suspect appears to have a solid alibi, will Ettie be able to find out who murdered the woman, or will the Amish man be charged over the murder?

Book 5
Amish Quilt Shop Mystery

Amish woman, Bethany Parker, finally realizes her dream of opening her own quilt shop. Yet only days after the grand opening, when she invites Ettie Smith to see her store, they discover the body of a murdered man.

At first Bethany is concerned that the man is strangely familiar to her, but soon she has more pressing worries when she discovers her life is in danger.

Bethany had always been able to rely on her friend, Jabez, but what are his true intentions toward her?

Connect with Samantha Price at:

samanthaprice333@gmail.com
http://twitter.com/AmishRomance
http://www.samanthapriceauthor.com
http://www.facebook.com/SamanthaPriceAuthor

60068737R00100

Made in the USA
Lexington, KY
25 January 2017